Latiful Islam Shibli, is a famous Bangladeshi poet and songwriter. In the early '90s, he composed a lot of beautiful heart-touching lyrics, which created a special place in the hearts of the music lovers of not only '90s but of modern age as well. Later on, he became one of the bestseller novelists in Bengali literature. Most of his novels are based on true events related to politics, history, romance and spirituality, which made him unique and different from other novelists.

Apart from that, he is a screenwriter, a columnist, an actor, a singer, a model and a fashion icon for the future generations of Bangladesh.

He is continuously fighting for freedom of speech and social justice.

Kazi Golam Hakkani Kita,

I can still find our childhood in your smile.

# Latiful Islam Shibli

## THE SEIZE

The Fight to Seize a Secret
City Within the City

AUSTIN MACAULEY PUBLISHERS™

LONDON · CAMBRIDGE · NEW YORK · SHARJAH

A CIP catalogue record for this title is available from the British Library.

ISBN 9781528985086 (Paperback)
ISBN 9781528985093 (ePub e-book)

www.austinmacauley.com

First Published (2021)
Austin Macauley Publishers Ltd
25 Canada Square
Canary Wharf
London
E14 5LQ

# Chapter 1

"Now I understand why you wanted to bring me to this jungle so far from the city."

"Why would you think like that? Your poet just wanted to see you in nature, wanted to know you or nature – who is more primitive."

"Very good, but I am seeing that the poet himself is becoming primitive, and gradually he is becoming barbaric too."

"What are you saying? I am being barbaric with you?"

"Yes, off course! This is my hand that you are holding right now, and I can feel the primitiveness in your touch…"

Jennifer looked at poet Anindya Akash's eyes deeply. In Jennifer's eyes were the coldness of the North Pole, and in her lively smile, the Saharan sandstorm. Poet Anindya Akash could feel the intensity of both. So far he was holding Jennifer's hand in his hand, but now when he tried to pull his hand away, he discovered that she's gripping it with a lot of power. The punishment of invisible humiliation sent a cool wave through him.

In order to lighten this moment of discomfort, the poet said with a fake smile, "The touch of the poet is like the life-giving wand of a fairy goddess, whose touch awakens the woman and nature."

"Your words are true, poet. But not the touch of the poet's hand, but his poetry awakens nature and the woman. I enjoy the touch of your poetry rather than the touch of your hand…"

Anindya Akash feels he has been caught red-handed, his last one month's labour, hope and plans were shattered. However, Jennifer was not looking at him while talking. As if she gave this space to the poet so that he could hide himself.

In the same way, the judges declare death by hiding their feelings of emotions, Jenny said with distant eyes, "You cannot touch a woman innocently with a body of blood and flesh, oh poet! Touching her body without touching the woman's mind is savagery."

Anindya Akash was confined to an overwhelming fascination. So far, seven books of poems had been released by him. In the last three years, he wrote about three hundred poems and all three of his books had been dedicated to Jennifer. Jennifer was fascinated by poems. This charm of her was genuine, as genuine as Anindya Akash's poems. But Akash could not match Jennifer's appreciation of poetry with her feelings for himself in any way. Anindya Akash wanted to get her by impressing her. He had impressed her all right, but still, he could not conquer Jennifer's heart.

The poet had come to know that charm was not the only way to win one's heart, but there was something else. He did not have any clue about that yet. This was a great pain for the poet.

And Jennifer's speciality was here, she did not move a hair outside her faith. Anindya Akash was trapped in such a difficult situation, in a primitive fascination. But he was sure that he loved Jennifer, right now he could give his life for her. But he could not say that to Jennifer so easily. Poetry was what he used as a way to say this. And Jennifer knew that was what the poet was telling her in the poem, all of it was true. But the rest was not true at all. Jennifer was not touched by what was not true. She had received this sensitivity about truth and falsehood from her family. Her father was a poet. He went to England, where he got acquainted with her mother, fell in love, and then married. Her mother was pure British, and her father, genuine Bangladeshi, and Jennifer was at the receiving end of both cultures. When she spoke pure and standard Bengali, there was no way to understand that she was born and grew up in England. Her poet father taught her literature. Along with Shakespeare, Byron, Blake, William Wordsworth, Milton, George Eliot and Robert Browning. He also made her read Rabindranath, Nazrul, Jibanananda Das, Al Mahmood, Shamsur Rahman, and Shaheed Kadri.

She had graduated from The University of Cambridge in literature. In England, she had read a lot of poetry from Bangladesh. She used to surround herself with Bengali songs and poems. She would find the latest text of contemporary poets and fiction writers in online blogs. Since then, the name of the poet Anindya Akash had attracted her. She was fascinated by his poetry. There was a regular chat between them in Messenger about Bengali literature, especially poetry. In the meantime, she received an offer from North South University to teach there, in the Department of English and Modern Language Faculty. Jennifer did not miss this opportunity to stay in Bangladesh. Her father also encouraged. Her father wanted to spend the last period of his life in Bangladesh. Her parents had been divorced for a long time. Her mother married again, and now she lived in France. Jennifer lived with her father. She grew up with her father's education and moral values and believed that sex was a sin without marriage. The belief had been deeply rooted as she grew up. For this reason, her British boyfriend called her 'Boring'. At this moment, Martin's expression while saying 'Boring' was hanging in the face of Anindya Akash. Suddenly Jennifer felt like laughing out loud. She tried to hide her smile. The brave men's helpless face while being with a boring woman felt very funny to Jennifer. But Martin was a lot easier, he was straightforward about his feelings. The same cannot be said about Anindya Akash, but Jennifer could read him. Her feelings about the poet, while chatting online or talking on the phone from a distance, stumbled on the first day of the meeting, when she knew that the poet's real name was Abul Khayer Paramanik. Jennifer was surprised to hear that the name given by his father was not considered cool in the literary society. She did not like the efforts of the authors to write with a pseudo-name, because she felt that it was like dusting off the rich smell of soil. However, she understood that the poets did not break any rules. Besides, the life that was found in the poetry of Anindya Akash, the rage of protest and the music of humanity's freedom made everything else unimportant.

Suddenly, a muffled sound brought them to reality. The time that was pressed with tension became fluid. They looked back to find the source together.

After a lot of searching, the poet had found this place. They walked through the east side of Bhawal National Park in Gazipur for about half an hour, then crossed the boundary of the park. After walking a little more through the shallow forest, a branch river could be seen. The river moved in a snake-like pattern; creating a strange landscape in the forest, then suddenly disappearing again inside the green. The poet did not say anything to Jennifer before to surprise her. The jungle was always a favourite for Jennifer. She was impressed when she heard about a jungle so close to Dhaka City. After the walk, they arrived, and the view was literally breathtaking. Jennifer's fascination made the poet bold.

The place was very isolated. People do not often come here. Even on reaching the banks of the river, they could not even find any sign of walking. Through the dense bushes, they had walked, and spider webs and bird feathers had clung to their dresses. The poet had brought a plastic mat, Jennifer's favourite chips, coffee flax, and water bottle in the bag on his shoulder. Jennifer was feeling a strange love for the poet after seeing how this madness fascinated her. Poet Anindya Akash could feel that. The silence of this jungle and the desire for this woman sitting beside him was creating a storm inside him. He had held Jennifer's hand for the first time today. But he could not guess that her reaction would be so weird. Her logic was eating him from inside now. Her silence and the natural solitude of the place together made him feel like as if he was being whipped by an invisible hand.

The sound that came suddenly became a saviour for the poet. He became very active for a short time to soften the stifling situation quickly. Both of them were sure that they heard an unusual sound. There is no way of ignoring the sound in this situation. The two stood up. They were sitting on the mat inside the long, dense grass. Except for the front, where the river was flowing, they were cut off from the world. They were looking at each other, listening intently. The sound became more pronounced. The sound was coming from near the bend of the river where it disappeared again in the jungle. It came nearer, and it was clear now that someone was crying. Another voice, like an imperceptible threat, accompanied the sobbing. The poet was confused with an unknown threat. He could not understand exactly what to do right now. He was in a lonely place away from the locality, and there was an attractive woman like Jennifer with him. He did not think about the matter of their own safety because of the excitement that came from the probability of being alone with Jennifer.

"It seems like something very serious."

Jennifer's words made the poet jump back to reality. "Yes, I think so."

Along with the quiet screams, the voices of two people could be heard now.

Jennifer said, "Let's look a little further."

The poet agreed reluctantly. No weakness could be expressed in front of Jennifer.

They advanced silently and very carefully through the tall grass along the banks of the river. After walking for a bit, the poet looked back and saw that Jennifer had stopped. She looked like a statue, staring closely at a bush to their left.

Poet Anindya Akash whispered her name, 'Jennifer'. There was no response. The poet called again, 'Jenny?' Jenny did not respond this time too, standing still in the same way. He came forward, following the gaze of her. After coming closer to her and looking at the bust, suddenly the poet became paralysed.

Twisting itself on the trunk of a small Gajari tree, with an aggressive stance, a giant black snake stared at them. Growing up in a village, Anindya Akash identified the terribly poisonous snake at once. Monocle cobra.

This snake was one of the biggest threats in watery areas like this. The time seemed to stand still. A light wind blew over them, scratched the grass blades with a faint sound, but none of them could move. Both were afraid that the snake would attack as soon as they moved. Desire makes people go blind. So there was no thought about the dangers of this place in Anindya Akash's head. The screaming came again, even more, audible now.

It was as if the snake had mesmerised Jennifer.

Slowly grabbing Jennifer's wrist, the poet brought his lips to her ear and whispered, "Let's go, Jenny."

Slowly, they stepped away from the snake's sight, as if admitting defeat.

Now every step through the thick grass sent a wave of panic through them. The whole grassland was making sounds like a thousand snakes were trapped inside a dark room.

The sound could be heard very clearly now, and the fear of snakes was quickly replaced by another fear. They had reached the farthest end of the grassland by crossing about a few hundred feet. A little bit was visible on the other side. It turned out that some people were moving out there. They approached a little further, then hid behind a dense bush. Then they pushed the sharp leaves of grass aside wearily and realised that they were going to be witnesses of a murder within a few minutes.

# Chapter 2

Jahangir was caught from Daudkandi. He was unconscious after drinking a bottle of drugged coke, so there was no major hassle when catching him. It was important to keep him alive to ensure his death. He was brought to Narayanganj's Shitalaksha Char from Daudkandi. After one day, a sand carrier trawler had brought him to Kaliganj.

Through the unnavigable marshlands of Kaliganj, Jahangir had been taken to this place, Bankhoria. This was the area of Shaheed Chairman. If Joydevpur, Kaliganj and Kapasia were the three points of a triangle, then inside this triangle was extensive wetlands and croplands. The western plains merged with the back of the Bhawal National Park. The area was literally deserted. This triangle was controlled by Shaheed Chairman. There was not much crime locally, so the police were totally free of tension. Shaheed Chairman was the only person who had anything to do with trials and judging. No one except a few knew about the atrocities that were committed behind the plain silence of this region.

Shaheed Chairman did not get directly involved in any such events. But today's job was very special. In the last ten years, he had to do this job only three times.

The responsibility of this type of work could not be left to anyone. His main job was the rowing of the boat, which did not go well with his current position and personality. Today was a sunny day, but from the moment he entered this side of the marsh, Shaheed Chairman was feeling a little cold. This feeling was not familiar to him. He was 65 years old, but it was just a number to him until this day. The past history of Shaheed Chairman has been completely covered by his current popular image. For the last thirty years, he had been the chairman of this region. If he wanted, he could become the chairman of the Upazila, or even MP. But Shaheed Chairman did not cross his limits. No criminal dared to rise up in this whole triangle, only because of him.

The most dangerous murderer in the history of Bangladesh was Imdu of this Kaliganj. He emerged through the help of JSD in politics. He used to kill people and hang them openly. He killed a child in front of his mother, even played football with the severed head of some unfortunate guy. Shaheed Chairman was the youngest collaborator of his gang. Imdu had been hanged to death, many of his people were murdered by the opposition or jailed for a long time. Shaheed came out of jail just after two years because of his young age. He did not return to the underworld in the same way ever again, but all the criminals in the region were still afraid of him. Under his chairman's guise, he was in charge of an invisible kingdom like an undeclared sovereign.

When the major changes took place in the city, the news came to Shaheed chairman at first. He did not like to do these things anymore. Every time the news arrived, a strange sensation spread throughout his body. While coming through the bill, small mounds in the ground could be seen on the west side. If someone looked closely, he could see that some of the mounds are still visibly swelled like a fish's belly. The number of poor people who have lost their lives forever under these high grounds is so numerous, even Shaheed Chairman himself could not remember. He was waiting for the passengers after seeing them get down from the boat. Today was the day of a lot of discomforts. He could feel Goosebumps forming on his body now and then. He could not even recognise himself, and he did not want to stay in this place for a moment longer. The air was so heavy here that it was uncomfortable to breathe. They were taking a lot of time to complete the job today. It should not take much time. The life of Shaheed Chairman had been stuck in a silent cycle of change. The Last time he was here, it was Jahangir who called him. Jahangir picked up Subrata Kundu and brought him here. Kundu prayed so pitifully to be shot to death.

Jahangir did not keep that request. He buried him alive. This is the rule of this business. Jahangir did not break the rules. Jahangir's farsightedness was blurred by the sands of power. If that rule was broken on that day, it could have been easy for him to die today. Was Jahangir crying like Kundu? If Shaheed Chairman could see that with his own eyes, he could have solved the equation about the decision of fate. Shaheed Chairman broke the rules for himself, and he was surely going to witness that math of breaking the rules. But why were they so late today! Would David keep Jahangir's last request?

# Chapter 3

Johnny was digging the hole with a spade. Kibria raised loose soil with his hand, while Aslam was monitoring them. None of them had any experience digging a pit.

Before starting work, Johnny had asked if the pit would be shaped like a grave.

Aslam shouted in reply, "Did we bring a dead body for which you want to dig a grave?"

Johnny felt embarrassed by asking such a foolish question. So, he decided to dig a square-shaped hole. Aslam ordered that the hole should be deep enough up to their chest height. Jahangir was paying a lot of attention to their work. His hands were tied behind his back. He had been in this position for the past two days. His hands were so tightly bound that he could not move them at all. Blood circulation has stopped in them, so he could not feel them at all.

Jahangir was sitting on a high mound nearby. Although there was a feeling of drowsiness, his nerves were fully aware, and he knew what was going to happen within a few minutes. Several times he had tried to find the place where he had buried Subrata Kundu. There was no way to distinguish anything among the grass. This is a place where people like Subrata, Jahangir and David came only twice. The purpose of the first time is to kill, and the last time is to die. And today was the last day of Jahangir and the first day of David. Aslam, Johnny and Kibria were paying a lot of attention to the task at hand. And Jahangir was watching their work even more closely. The depth of the hole had already dropped to knee-level. Kundu did not get much time. The pit for him was already open before he was taken here. Shaheed Chairman had already made all the arrangements. Compared to Kundu,

Jahangir was getting a lot of time. Who knew how long it would take to dig from knee to waist, then to chest level deep. Jahangir could not think of how David could handle all these hassles with these inexperienced people. Since David left the boat, he did not seem to have any focus on anything. He was standing a little away from them, talking to someone on the phone with a lot of attention. Only Jahangir knew who he was talking to now.

After finishing the talk, David stood like a statue facing the river. Anyone might think he had no interest in what was going on with Jahangir. He just glanced once and measured the depth of their hole with his eyes. Jahangir could never tolerate this thing. Whoever you are, you need to pay attention to Jahangir. David should be aware of this, so maybe that is why he was ignoring Jahangir.

Jahangir was slowly waking up inside. The hole was now as deep as Johnny's waist. Jahangir was looking stubbornly at David, a murderer's look in his eyes. Suddenly, turning back to the river, David looked directly at Jahangir. He was a little surprised inside. The fire and hatred in Jahangir's eyes touched for a moment. Jahangir lowered his eyes down. David came forward and sat next to Jahangir. Both of them were silently watching the hole being dug. The grass leaves were whispering in the gentle breeze, a lonely magpie called away somewhere without the whole world was silenced except the wet sound of spades hitting the soil. David asked in a very soft voice:

"Want a smoke?"

Remaining silent for a while, Jahangir said, "Okay."

David pulled out a cigarette packet from his pocket, lit one, and took three puffs. Then he put it on Jahangir's lips. Jahangir filled up his lungs with a long draw of cigarette smoke.

There was a strange change inside Jahangir as he was smoking the cigarette with utmost satisfaction. Nicotine's poison brought into himself thoughts like normal people. Being emotionally attacked, suddenly he started to cough. David removed the cigarette from his lips. Jahangir took some time before stopping his cough. David kept on smoking the remaining cigarette. Johnny's waist was now below the hole. David planted the cigarette in Jahangir's lips again. After Jahangir dragged a long breath full of cigarette smoke, David pulled it away and smoked for a while. When he tried to put the cigarette between Jahangir's lips again, he shook his head. David finished the rest of the cigarette alone. The digging was fast now as the bottom of the hole was soft.

"Will you keep a request of mine?"

David knew what Jahangir would ask him now. So he asked in an indirect way, "Are you scared?"

Jahangir did not respond to the insult and said in a desperate voice, "Do not bury me alive, David. Shoot me instead."

Both of them looked at the river. A long sigh came out of David's chest for some unknown reason. Jahangir could hear it from beside him.

"Rules cannot be broken."

"Then make new rules."

"That is really hard. I do not have the power to change karma!"

Grinding his teeth, Jahangir cursed in a very tranquil voice and said, "If you cannot change the rules, what will you do with this power and empire?" Then he cursed again about doing something with David's mother and continued to abuse. In these cases, David became very calm and tried to understand Jahangir's move. He stared at the angry face of Jahangir. Jahangir wanted to enrage him so that he shoots him right now. The three of them stopped their work to look at David and Jahangir. David noticed that the depth of the hole was now equal to Johnny's chest height. Jahangir was still abusing David's mother, unspeakably. After a while, he stopped and started to pant.

David called, "Aslam!"

Aslam came running.

David gave a signal.

Aslam grabbed Jahangir's hair and dragged him towards the hole. Jahangir started to curse again. When he reached near the hole, he cried out loudly, "Stop, stop! I have to tell you something for the last time. Listen to me, David."

Hearing the request, Aslam turned to look at David. David gestured him to stop. Aslam made Jahangir stand on the edge of the hole. He would fall in the hole even with a little push. David walked slowly and came to stand facing Jahangir.

Jahangir's face was contorted with the fear of death.

"What do you want to say?"

As an answer, Jahangir spat audibly on David's face. His last attempt to enrage David did not bear any fruit. David wiped his face with his shirtsleeve, then threw Jahangir into the hole with a kick on his chest.

# Chapter 4

"We have to save that person."

Jennifer whispered from behind the densely growing grass.

"We cannot do anything by ourselves now. I do not have any number of police stations in the neighbourhood. Even if I had, it would take a long time for the police to reach here. That man would be surely dead by then."

The poet could feel a strange fragrance coming from Jennifer's body. The scent did not seem to be just a perfume. It seemed that it was the smell of the jungle itself. Jenny was all but jumping up and down in excitement and tension.

"Then we have to do what we need to do quickly. This man's life must be saved."

Jenny's words hit the poet solidly. What was she saying! He whispered fiercely, "Why do we have to do that? What can we do?"

"Don't you see that a helpless man is being buried alive? What should we do now?"

Jenny looked at him with hard eyes. The poet understood the meaning of that look, so he said in an attempt to pacify her, "Listen, Jenny. As far as I can understand, they are ruthless organised criminals. We're going to be witness to one of their murders, and do you think they will keep any proof of their crime? If they found out about us being here, they will bury us in the same hole along with that man. Why can't you understand such a simple thing, Jenny?"

"The man is still alive, and there is no one else to save the man except us. A helpless innocent person is being killed before my eyes, and I am sitting quietly-do I have to spend the rest of my life with such a shame?"

"We're helpless, Jenny."

"No, we are not more helpless than that person."

"Do you want to save another's life by endangering your life?"

Jenny was surprised to hear these words and just stared at the poet.

"Then why do you write these things in your poetry?"

"What do you mean, Jenny?"

"I mean, why do you write poetry about the liberation of people, the rights of the oppressed people? Why did you say in poetry 'human' that…

"'My friend, to keep you alive

My heart will turn into a wall

An obstacle

Where a million bullets of the assassin will be resisted

In this chest…'

"This is where you wrote about saving other's life by endangering your own life. Why did you say such a thing, poet?"

"You cannot confuse poetry with reality, Jenny."

"What does that mean? Everything that you have said in your poems, are lies?"

Poet Anindya Akash could not find an answer. What is the answer to this question?

He mumbled, "It's not like that. They are not lies."

"I too believe so. I believe in every letter of your poems. Believe in recklessly. Perhaps I believe them even more than you. You do not even know how much strength and courage your poetry gives me. And now you will see how strong your poetry really is. I'm going to save that helpless man."

Holding her hand tightly, Poet Anindya Akash desperately said, "Jenny, please don't be crazy!"

Jenny pulled her hand with a flitting smile and said, "You say that poetry means craziness, and you alone are responsible for that."

Standing up from the crouching position, she rushed from the grassland to the bank of the river, ignoring the poet's desperate plea from her behind, "Jenny, please don't…"

# Chapter 5

As soon as Jahangir fell into the hole, Johnny, Kibria and Aslam started pitching the soil on him. And just at that moment, they saw a girl running towards them. They were startled. 9mm pistols appeared in all of their hands immediately. Aslam, Johnny and Kibria moved away and took positions in three places.

Although they pulled their pistols out at first as a reflex action, the sight of the girl made them lower their hands down. Now everyone was looking at the other's eyes. They wanted to be sure if the girl was alone or someone else was with her. Jennifer stood in front of David. Aslam rushed forward with his pistol, and asked with a grim face, "What are you doing? Where are you from? Why are you here, and who sent you?"

Jennifer was wearing a pair of blue jeans and a loose white shirt. A scarf was on her neck, and her eyes were covered with golden frame glasses. The situation did not improve when Aslam charged a five and a half feet tall girl with his rude questions. Jenny understood at first glance that the man wearing the cap was in charge of everyone here. So she ignored Aslam and looked straight at David. "Search her bag, Aslam," commanded David. Aslam snatched the Armani handbag from Jennifer's shoulder and emptied the contents on the ground. There were several womanly things inside the bag and an iPhone. Kibria picked up the phone and handed it over to David.

"Don't worry about me, please. I will tell you everything."

David tried to open the phone and saw that it was locked. Jennifer said, "I was here with my friend, to visit the National Park. Don't know when I lost my way. When I saw that you were going to bury this man alive, I could not hold myself back. My conscience tells me to save this man…"

Johnny, Kibria and Aslam did not expect to hear this lecture, so they glanced at each other sheepishly. A grin spread across Johnny's face. Jahangir's eyes bulged, jaw hanging down. After being thrown into the hole, Johnny came down and bound Jahangir's legs. Standing in the holes in the bound feet, he thought at this moment that this woman must be an angel from the heavens, here to save his life. Jahangir did not hope of surviving his life since being caught, because he knew his fate had been determined. But now he wanted to live strongly.

Jennifer said to David, "Please do not kill the man, please let him go."

David handed Jennifer the phone without replying to her request and said, "Unlock this phone."

Jennifer used her thumb to unlock the phone and gave it to David. He checked her call history and Messenger inbox quickly.

The last conversation was with someone named poet Anindya Akash. Suddenly the phone started to ring, startling everyone. The name that appeared on the screen was – poet Anindya Akash.

Everyone was alert because of the tension. The phone kept ringing. David put his pistol's barrel on Jennifer's forehead and said, "Please turn on the speaker and talk normally. Otherwise, I'll shoot him." He handed the phone to Jennifer. Jennifer noticed that David used the term 'please' when talking to her.

Hiding behind the tall grass leaves, poet Anindya Akash could not hear any words from them clearly. But he could guess that whatever happens, these people should be given the message that Jenny was not alone here. She came here with someone. Jenny's last location record will be in the phone's navigation. In these cases, the criminals generally switched off the phone. So, when he saw from a distance that they were handling Jennifer's phone, he quickly decided to call. The most important aspect of Anindya's character was that he was never angry. His head could work very methodically and worked even better than usual when he was faced with danger.

Anindya Akash could hear the phone's sound clearly from his position. He could also see that four pistols were staring hungrily at Jenny. She received the call and said, "Hello."

"Oh, Jenny, honey, where are you? I am looking for you for so long. Listen, I caught four golden butterflies for you. I will put them in your hair and take some pictures. I might put one of them on your nose, too, hahaha…anyway, where are you right now? Are you okay?"

"I am okay, baby. Go back to the resort restaurant and wait for me. I will be back soon."

"Hurry up, baby. Your poet is dying for you…"

Jenny disconnected the call.

She was totally amazed at the cool-headedness of poet Anindya Akash.

Their suspicions about Jenny were almost gone now, but not totally. They were a people of a certain lifestyle who live in suspicion. They could not let her go so easily just because she was here coincidentally.

Jenny started requesting again, "Please don't kill this innocent, helpless man. Let him go."

Jahangir was a notorious and reckless gang leader of Dhaka city. Calling him innocent was like a big joke to the others. They just stood there, glancing at each other's face.

David asked sarcastically, "Do you know him? I don't think so. How can you be so sure that he is innocent?"

"No, I don't know him. But I know that an oppressor is never a human, and the oppressed is always human."

David got a little shocked hearing her words.

Unlike Jahangir, David did not come up from the slums of Keraniganj. He has studied at a Public University. His major was Political science, and his introduction to the armed student politics also took place there. He was touched by the woman's strong words in front of four armed men. But he hid his emotions and asked again, "Does he look like a human to you?"

"Of course! He is a human, an innocent and helpless man."

Again, her words struck David the same way it did previously. If Jahangir was oppressed, then did she mean that David was the oppressor?

Aslam was starting to lose his temper, and said, "Boss, what's the point of wasting these words? Let me put this girl in the same hole with Jahangir!"

David did not show any sign of hearing him. The girl has made a subtle attack on his personality, and he wanted to answer her. "His name is Jahangir," David said. "You must have read about him in the newspapers—Jahangir of Keraniganj. Even two days ago, this whole city was under his control. He has killed and dumped the body of at least a hundred men. If given a chance, he won't hesitate to kill all of us right now. How can you call him a human being?"

"As long as he had the power to kill another human, maybe he was not a human. But just look at his eyes now, he is standing in front of death and trembling in fear. He is nothing but a human now. This man needs to live because he needs to repent. Give him that chance, give him his life. He will burn in the fire of his redemption and become a new person. Give him that chance...please."

Suddenly Jahangir started to cry loudly as if Jenny's words have touched him too. Not a notorious, murderous gang leader now, he was just a helpless human being.

"David, you are like my brother. Please give me a single chance. I will retire from everything. I will leave the country, and you will never see me again. Please give me my life, please...I beg you..."

David stared at him, surprised. He could not believe that this is the same Jahangir who used to terrorise the whole of Dhaka. That man was crying like a child now. Jenny followed his stare and said, "Give him a chance, please."

Aslam could not hold his temper any more. He shouted, "will you stop this nonsense, boss? We are getting late..."

Johnny told Jahangir to be silent with a slap. Kibria stood up with a spade in his hands, ready to pour the soil into the hole. Jenny was desperately trying her best. She diverted David's whole focus on herself, saying, "There is only one difference between humans and monsters, a human can forgive, but monsters cannot…"

David looked at Jenny's eyes steadily. Like throwing a challenge, Jenny said, "If you want to kill this person because he has killed a hundred, then who can tell that by killing this man you won't commit your own century? Please, forgive at least once in life, please forgive him and become a human."

Aslam shouted, "Silence, woman! Boss, just tell me once…"

But David and Jenny had forgotten their surroundings, and they were fighting a war with words.

David, with a steely and cold voice, asks, "Don't I look like a human?"

"Not until you are a forgiver."

"What is the benefit for me if I become human? The world is run by monsters, after all."

"Man's love is available when people are human, and hate is only for inhumanity."

"I live in a world where there are no humans, so I have neither the need nor the chance to get the love of a human being. If I leave this world today, my own people will hate me."

"It is Allah Who created the earth that belongs to you, although sometimes there Satan reigns. Satan's heart is hard, he does not know how to forgive. Forgiveness is the quality of Allah. He who forgives, is the friend of Allah. The one who receives the quality of forgiveness gets enormous spiritual strength. You will achieve that power, and nobody will be able to survive in front of your power."

David threw out his last challenge and asked Jenny, "Will you love a person like me?"

Without any hesitation, Jenny answered, "If you are forgiving!"

"Are you sure?"

Jenny replied in a firm voice, "Absolutely."

Jenny and David were looking at each other. Jahangir's cry was stopped now. Johnny, Kibria and Aslam were stunned; they could not imagine what was going to happen. Suddenly the environment drowned in a strange silence.

This was the first time that David broke the oldest rule of the underworld.

"Aslam."

"Yes, boss."

"Release Jahangir."

"Don't do this boss...Do not make this mistake, please don't do it."

David turned towards Aslam and. Aslam could not look back at his tough cold stare and retreat inside himself like a snail.

"Sorry boss...okay, boss..." Aslam mumbled and jumped in a hole. He took out a knife from his pocket and cut the strap on Jahangir's hands and legs.

Johnny and Kibria dragged him out of the hole. Jahangir, weeping and whispering, dived down on David's legs with gratitude. He threw himself on the ground and kissed David's shoes repeatedly.

"Thank you, David, I have become your slave for my life, because you saved my life today. I will leave this country; I will never come in front of you again."

Then he looked at Jennifer and said, "Thank You, mother..."

Slowly Jahangir started to walk backwards. Due to fear and panic, he kept on walking by one and two steps and continued to express his gratitude the whole time. Jahangir still could not believe his luck yet. Jahangir was very well aware of the underworld's rule about betrayal and disbelief. At any moment, David and his people could change and charge. Moving back safely to a safe distance, he started to run. Within a few moments, he was lost in the woods.

# Chapter 6

Poet Anindya Akash came out of the jungle. The sun had inclined towards the west; it was almost afternoon. The blue sky was covered in some places with torn clouds. A hungry-looking pit could be seen lying on the ground, dug not long ago. The poet looked at the hole. Somehow he felt that this hole had a hypnotic power. It was dragging him as if it wanted to catch new victims after losing one. It was staring at him fiercely, beckoning him. It was not for dead people, this hole wanted his victims alive. A dove was calling away somewhere. Something eerie was here in this place. This place might be the last address of many lost people from Dhaka city. Poet Anindya Akash was standing on the mounds of earth that were raised from the hole, and after surveying his surroundings, it occurred to him that this could be the ideal place to make someone disappear. Such a place could not be found anywhere else, so near to Dhaka.

Google was saying that when Joydevpur, Kapasia and Kaliganj held the three vertices of the triangle, this place was just in the middle of them. Maybe there are three police stations in those three areas. Therefore, it was normal for any police station to hesitate in taking responsibility for any incident that happens in this location.

Many of the people who get caught by the plain-clothed persons of the country's security organisations could not be found later anymore. Those who were kidnapped for ransom, rivalry and contact killings also disappeared forever. Many people vanished because of the internal collisions of the top terrorist godfathers, and they were also lost forever. Maybe this was the place, that dumping zone where the dead or living people were buried. Thinking about all these things, cold sweat started to cover his body. The place seemed to be too much silent now, making him uncomfortable. Even the dove that was calling from far away was not heard anymore.

The poet has suddenly noticed that in such a wild environment, not a lot of birds or other animal sounds could be heard, which was highly unlikely. He left the grassland behind and came to the edge of the river. The sun was declining towards the horizon.

Only a boat could be seen in the middle of the huge marshland. A single boatman was pulling the oars, causing it to move through the water. Jennifer was in that boat. The people did not take the risk to release her. She might have known their identity.

But whatever happened, it could not be denied that Jennifer had done an impossible job today. She really did save the man. Poet Anindya Akash knew very well about the strength of Jennifer's belief and honesty. And he also knew that it was not possible for any other person to harm a girl like Jennifer. But he could not find a reason why or match the conditions on which they had taken Jennifer. They would not do any harm to Jennifer, at least this much could be guessed from their body language. Now the only way to get those who had taken Jennifer away was to find the survivor. He knew who he was. Poet Anindya Akash looked at the boat for one last moment, a tiny dot in the vast marshland; before entering the jungle to find the man.

# Chapter 7

The water was shining like clear glass. Water Lily, Kesel and other unknown aquatic plants had made a dense jungle under the water surface, and small fishes were playing in them. A lot of fishes should be available in this bill, but the silent and secluded area did not have any sign of fishing boats or people. Aslam's phone continued to ring after every few minutes, creating a sweet melody when mixed with the sound of the oar cutting water. There was no sound anywhere else around them. Jennifer could feel a deep tension among the silent passengers of the boat. After a few minutes, the mobile phone in Aslam's hand rang again. After staring at the phone screen for several moments, he looked at David and called, "Boss." David was sitting on the head of the boat, distant from the others. He was looking at the horizon, a distant look in his eyes. Aslam's voice broke his trance.

Jennifer has made a rough idea of who these people were and how dangerous their nature was. She had realised that Jahangir had accepted his defeat, and this man named David had emerged in his place. Jennifer's ex-boyfriend Martin had a friendship with a gang of the Tottenham area in London. She saw that sex, drugs, Rock n Roll Hip Hop, violence, arms and money had mixed with the flavour of power, creating an eclectic mix of fashion and culture for the gang. But seeing David's work, it seemed to her that they were part of more serious and deep action.

Meanwhile, she had understood a bit about David. Maybe that's why she was not having any bad feelings about him. David's eyes looked suspicious, not greedy. Jennifer had understood the inherent power of seeing inside David. When needed, he looked with quick firmness. This quickness was not normal, and in his eyes looked like two dark pits at that moment. As soon as Aslam called him, David looked at Jennifer first, as if wondering if he could talk in front of her. The phone was ringing. Aslam simply said, "DG."

DG must be a short name or designation for someone, Jennifer thought. What name can that be? If it was a designation, then the first thought that came to her mind was Director-General.

With the impression of reluctant doubt and deep thought, David said, "Hello."

Whoever it was on the other side of the phone, he must surely be someone honourable. David could be seen listening to him and nodding. After a while, he only said, "Thank You." Jennifer guessed that the person called 'DG' congratulated him. David was silent, intent on hearing the person's words. For the first time, Jennifer took a good look at David. His complexion might have been fair once, but now it was burnt olive. He was wearing Blue jeans and light check shirt with folded sleeves, lightweight boots on the legs and a golf cap on his head. David's clothing and speaking style were completely different than his other three companions. There was a certain type of leading personality in him that deserved to be respected. David probably liked to use his stare more instead of talking. His last word before cutting the call was 'OK'. That meant he used only three words to talk to DG, thought Jennifer. Jennifer looked away from him just before he ended his conversation on the phone. The boat stopped beside the banks of the marshland. As David was sitting in the front, he got down first. Jennifer got down after him. She had to stand twice and sit down because the boat was rocking. Seeing it, David held the boat steady with his hands. Some other person might have offered a hand to Jennifer, but he did not do anything like that. Everyone else got down after Jennifer. The boatman bound the boat to a small stump on the ground, then came to David. David was waiting for him with a small smile. He offered his hand to the man and said, "Thanks for everything, Shaheed Bhai."

Shaheed Chairman's expressionless face became flushed for a second. This was the first time that someone called him "Bhai" and gave him thanks after the job was done. Could it be that David was breaking the rules of his world? Shaheed Chairman still did not know that David had let Jahangir go. And all he knew about the girl is that she lost her way and appeared there accidentally. When David tried to pull his hand away after shaking hands with Shaheed Chairman, he saw that the man was holding his hand tightly. It seemed to him that the silent, white-bearded person with a philosopher's face wanted to say something. Pulling him closer, the man whispered to David so that the others could not hear him and said, "Everyone works on this line using their heads. No one can stay for a long time because they don't use their heart. Remember that."

After that, he looked deeply in David's eyes for a few moments. Then he lowered his head and kissed David's hand. With this token, he proved that his loyalty was towards David from now on.

Johnny and Kibria were walking in front of the party, a few steps ahead. Aslam was just behind David and Jennifer. They had to follow a walking road to get to the main road from the side of the marshland. Three phones were constantly ringing. Jennifer was feeling anxious inside. Nobody was telling her anything, but she knew that she was a captive in their hands now. She just could not understand what was going to happen to her. They were walking through a dense mango garden. The shadow of the huge mango trees made the place look unreal even in this daylight, as if from the pages of a horror story. After crossing the garden, there was a broken road. There was a lot of holes on the road, red bricks and gravels could be seen here and there. The nearly abandoned road led to Dhaka-Mymensingh Highway in about one and a half kilometres. From this distance, highway traffic could be seen as a blur.

As soon as she stepped on the broken road, Jennifer was surprised.

About a dozen jeeps and fifty to sixty people suddenly appeared. Jennifer was shocked because the scene appeared in front of her after crossing a small bend in the street. Seeing their group of five, there was a buzz among the other party. After that, the closer they went, the more silent the entire environment became. Even a few days ago, nobody knew David's name. But today everyone knew him, although not by the face. They were surrounded by the group in a more or less D-shape position. Jennifer could feel the tension in the air. They were all armed. Some had Shotguns in their hands. However, they were keeping those arms horizontal to their body, as if in an attempt to hide them from view. Everyone else was concealing their arms in pockets or some other way. In these attempts of hiding their weapons, there was a hidden message – a message of respect. It could be compared to the teenager's attempt to hide cigarettes if some elder suddenly came in front of them. David had earned this respect today. Everyone present here knew what he had done. Jennifer could guess that. And the thought made her ashamed.

The first person who came forward was Mirza of Savar. He had a paralysed hand, the result of an opposition gang's stabbing in his school life. Everyone called him Tunda (Paralysed) Mirza behind his back. His main business is to land seizing, garments, extortion in factories, etc. He was also the monopoly owner of the sand business in this area and an underground Yaba factory. If Savar was a money-making machine, then Tunda Mirza was the sole proprietor of that machine. Even the local MP's winning or defeat depended on Mirza's decision. David talked to him before getting into the job. Now Mirza came forward and respectfully took David's hand in his own, then kissed it. Everyone else recognised David at once.

The capital city of Dhaka was confined within a secret circle, which had five main points. Tongi, Rupganj, Godnail, Keraniganj and Savar. If someone added these five points according to the scale, a pentagon formed. Whoever had control of this pentagon was the invisible ruler of Dhaka.

After Savar's Tunda, Motahar from Keraniganj came forward and said, "Bhai." He also kissed David's hand. Then Shukchan of Rupganj, Ranga from Godnail and lastly Tongi's Joynal Maker came to do the same.

Jennifer became a witness to a secret coup. David was not looking like the new underworld boss of Dhaka, but like a religious leader or saint at this moment. After the heads of the five main points, everyone else came one by one, filled with devotion towards David, and kissed him in hand.

Man is a worshiper by nature. He wants to worship anything or anyone more powerful than him or who has the power to show him mercy. Be that a rock or a hill or the moon, the sun, a river, a thunder, a fantasy monster or a powerful man, his instincts will lead him to worship it. Only a few people know about these hidden mysteries of human character weakness. There is a group among those few persons who guide that instinct to the worship of God, or towards Allah. Another group uses that instinct to worship the image or statues in the shrines. And another group entirely denies these two groups. They denied this worshipping nature as the 'intoxication of opium', but they also made huge statues of Stalin and Lenin. That is, they also could not come out of the power of that instinct.

Looking at David, who was busy accepting the loyalty of his people, Jennifer wondered how he would use this loyalty. Kibria came in front of her and motioned her to follow him. Her heart started to beat fast with an unknown fear. But Jennifer understood that Kibria was actually following David's orders. So she kept quiet and followed him. A shining black Lexus jeep stood a few steps away. Kibria opened the back door of the vehicle. Jenny went silently to sit in the car. The window glass was lowered down earlier, so she could see and hear everything from here too. Kibria stood beside her in an attempt to guard her. After everybody was finished shaking hands with David, Aslam came forward and started to talk to him. Kibria spoke to Jenny while looking at that direction,

"You must be dying to know who we are."

"I have guessed, but not the whole part."

34

"There is another type of government, do you know?"

Kibria waited for a few moments after asking the question. Then, as if understanding that Jennifer would not be able to answer his question, he said,

"There are two types of government. One is the governmental government, and another is private."

After a few moments of silence, he asked again,

"Do you know about the classification of law?"

Again he answers his own question. "One is the government implemented law, and another is implemented privately."

Aslam was talking loudly to everyone, Jennifer and Kibria could hear him from the car.

Kibria said, "We work for that private government. Our government has changed today. But not in the way it was supposed to be. This is the first time that the rule was broken. What you call the governmental body, we call it a circle. If Jahangir were buried alive, then the circle would have been completed. Only because of you it didn't. You have created a problem without any solution. You have uttered some gibberish that changed our boss' mind."

Jenny did not have any discomfort or fear about that. She believed that even the worst person in the world had a right to live. She did nothing wrong. She wanted to say something logical in answer to Kibria's complaint but had to stop as Aslam had stopped and David started to speak.

"Ten ward commissioner of Dhaka city is yet to join with the circle. I hope that the situation will change as we enter the city. If it doesn't then, we'll have to fight to take control of Janata Tower. We have eight hours in our hand. Michaels will keep their eyes and ears closed in this time…"

Jenny asked in a whisper, "Who are Michaels?"

"We call them governmental government and its administration and media Michaels jokingly," Kibria answered her like an ideal teacher, then turned his attention towards David again.

"There will be a power cut off in the surrounding area of Janata Tower between 12 am to 3 am tonight," David was saying. "If by any chance there is any hassle, we'll have to work as silently as possible. But I am still hopeful that there will be some negotiations before anything happens. And if it doesn't, we will take the Janata Tower by any means."

David took a short break after speaking the words. His personality and expression were totally changed now. He said in a grave voice like a veteran general, "Are you ready?"

Everyone took out their weapons excitedly. They put the guns over their head and said unanimously, "Yes, boss."

# Chapter 8

Poet Anindya Akash began looking for Jahangir from that part of the jungle where he disappeared. It was almost impossible to find a man in this huge jungle. But he did not have any other way to find Jenny. Jenny's phone was switched off, which made the poet nervous. As his fear grew more intense, he searched for Jahangir more desperately. Many times he had stumbled in the jungle. There were many cuts and bruises in his body from brushing with thorns and sharp twigs. He could feel a burning sensation in those places of his body. However, he lost hope of finding her just before the evening and entered the National Park boundary.

When he reached the park's resort, darkness had come down to cover the Gazari forest. With tired depression, he entered the resort and sat in a chair at the restaurant. For some time, he tried to relax his body while keeping his eyes closed and thinking about the next thing to do. He had to make a report at the local police station. Although it was almost certain that the report would be in vain, nevertheless, it had to be done, because if there was any legal problem in the future, then it would be his backup.

The resort's restaurant remained busy almost throughout the whole year. This was an ideal place to spend some time with nature while not venturing too far from the city. Poet Anindya Akash asked the waiter for a sandwich, coffee and a bottle of water. Suddenly his eyes turned to the garden beside the restaurant and became still. Yes, he could remember that the man was wearing a light yellow shirt. It could be guessed from the posture of the man the poet was looking at right now that he was trying to keep himself hidden.

Without any hesitation, he stood up and went to that man's table.

Jahangir started as he pulled out a chair to sit in front of him.

"How are you feeling?"

"What?"

"I mean, how are you enjoying this light, air, greenery, the darkness in your new life?"

"New life? What do you mean?"

Jahangir asked with a cold, doubtful stare. The poet enjoyed playing with him. He motioned for the waiter to serve his food at this table.

"You must be really hungry. Please eat, don't worry about the bill. I'll pay."

Jahangir took the bottle from the table and emptied it without any hesitation. The poet called the waiter and ordered some more food and water.

"From now on, everything you enjoy in this world is a bonus, isn't it?"

This time Jahangir asked straightforward, "Are you with David?"

Anindya Akash understood that David was the leader of those people who tried to kill this person. So he did not answer clearly.

"No, I don't work for anyone. I am a poet. I belong to everyone."

The poet smiled as if trying to say that there was nothing to be afraid of him. He was not an enemy but a friend. Jahangir was eating the sandwich with utmost satisfaction. Anindya Akash stared at him. His love for Jennifer had turned into fear now. But that fear should not be expressed, that much he could understand. Poet Anindya Akash knew that love is nothing but a strong weakness, which should not be shown to anyone. However, this weakness had its own way of expressing itself, and it did that only in front of that person for whom the love was intended.

After eating, Jahangir again drank a lot of water. Comfortable tiredness was now engulfing him. He relaxed on the chair. The poet asked, "Why did they want to kill you?"

Jahangir straightened up.

"How did you know that?" He asked.

"The girl who saved your life today was my girlfriend. We've seen everything from our hidden position. You owe your life to her."

The feelings of surprise or gratefulness were not working for Jahangir right now, because he was in a trance. He stared bemusedly at Anindya Akash for some time, then moved forward to touch the poet's hand and said, "I can never repay you enough."

He was going to say something more, but the poet stopped him and said excitedly, "This is not the time for niceties. You must repay me. My girlfriend, who has saved your life, they have captured her, and she needs to be rescued. It's not possible without you. You'll now go to the local police station. We have two cases. You'll file a case against him on the attempt to murder, and I'll file the case of woman abduction. Then we'll catch them with the police force."

Jahangir's face slowly lit up with a crooked smile. Poet Anindya Akash started to feel irritated to see him laughing like that. He said with a sour tone, "How can you smile in a situation like this? You should be crying and thanking me."

Jahangir's expression changed as if he slowly woke up from a deep sleep hearing the accusation from the poet. He crossed his legs, locked Anindya Akash's eyes in a cold stare, and the poet suddenly understood that there was something slightly off.

"My name is Jahangir."

The poet tried to ignore his threatening manner, and said in a sarcastic tone, "Are you talking about the Mughal Emperor?"

"I am an emperor all right, but of Keraniganj. I am Jahangir of Keraniganj."

As soon as he heard the words, poet Anindya Akash felt a chill run through his spine, making him still. A month ago, swollen dead bodies of five powerful cadres working for the government were found in the Buriganga River. One of the survivors survived somehow from Jahangir's hand. He gave a detailed blood-curdling description of the murders that Jahangir committed in his own hands. The entire country was stunned. The government was in a tough position at that time because of the rising rate of criminal incidents. It was an open secret that Jahangir worked for the government. The media started to protest openly, and many other murder cases started to come into the light, every one of which was connected directly to Jahangir.

That Jahangir of Keraniganj was now sitting in front of him.

Though it seemed difficult to believe at first, the poet was having a feeling from the very beginning that he had seen this person somewhere before. There was no possibility of any mistake because he had seen this face in many newspapers a number of times. The hair was cropped short. In the newspapers, Jahangir had long hair and clean shaved face, but now without most of his hair gone and face covered with short beard, he was not that recognisable any more. But the poet had recognised him at last. This was Jahangir of Keraniganj for sure.

Jennifer had saved this murderer. Was she so much powerful? Or did she get this power of faith from Anindya Akash's poems? If that was the truth, then it was not Jennifer, but poet Anindya Akash's poetry who saved Jahangir's life.

Under pressure from the public opinion and media, the government removed its shelter from over Jahangir. Jahangir had served many projects of the government. During the elections in the metropolitan areas of Dhaka city, the MPs were the main sponsors of Jahangir, who took away the victory by overturning the polling results. Many of the ward commissioners were the direct disciples of Jahangir. Everything was going well. Jahangir was like a powerful weapon. But all the bodies that suddenly appeared in Buriganga – they reversed everything. An influential group of people who could not take advantage of this so far because of

Jahangir, they became active within the government. They enraged the media silently and told the government that the government's image would be bright if Jahangir were brought to justice. The beneficiaries would be in trouble because after the trial, the names of many high-profile people would come out as the sponsors of Jahangir. So Jahangir had to be removed as soon as possible.

The administration could not find Jahangir. But David found Jahangir all right. And the person who helped him was none other than the Home Minister, Comrade Dastagir.

"Oh my god…It's you! But I cannot imagine why did your opponent become so foolish to let you go?"

Jahangir answered,

"To punish me even more. I would die only once, but now I'll die every day, every hour I'll die. David didn't know it. But your girlfriend convinced him. And he also found out my weakness. But your girlfriend had made a mistake in recognising me."

"What is that?"

"She thought I would burn in the fire of repentance."

Jahangir left a sigh.

"But it is not repentance, but what burns me up is my self-esteem. I had to ask David for forgiveness begging on his feet, I had to live with his mercy. Being buried alive seemed very hard then, but I didn't know that losing my power, losing my kingdom and surviving on somebody's mercy would be harder than that. What's the point of this survival?"

The poet could not have any advantage with this disappointed Jahangir. Without his help, Jennifer could not be rescued. So to provoke Jahangir, the poet said desperately, "What are you saying, Jahangir? Has this world been made to be ruled by sinners like us? Once you did not have the power, then you did. Today, it's true that you lost it, but who knows, you might get that power again tomorrow. I am with you."

Hearing the last words of the poet, Jahangir said with a mocking smile, "Who are you to get me my power back again!"

The poet asked in a serious face, "Do you still not understand who I am?"

"No, I don't. I don't know who you are."

"I am a poet. My name is poet Anindya Akash. My girlfriend is Jennifer, Jenny; who has saved your life today. Did she save you with arms or power? Tell me?"

Jahangir remained silent.

"Why are you not answering me? Speak!"

"No."

"Then how did she save you?"

"By telling some very expensive things."

"Now listen to who I am. Jennifer learned those expensive words by reading my poems. My poetry taught her how to be brave. How to stand beside the helpless people? How to stand in front of death and sing the joys of life? And that's what saved you. You were not saved by Jennifer; you were saved by the poet Anindya Akash's poems. I've saved you. Do you understand now, who I am! How strong is my power?"

When the poet Anindya Akash was saying these words, he became a true poet. He said these words with the power of his faith, just as Jennifer did when standing face-to-face with David. The power of the poet's words touched Jahangir. For a while, Jahangir could not help but remain silent. The poet was eagerly looking at his face. Jahangir said, "What do you want?"

"I want my girlfriend back."

"I don't have the power to bring her back. And somehow it occurs to me that David did not capture your girlfriend by force."

"Why do you think so?"

"Because she told David that if he forgave me, she would love David."

Being excited, the poet asked, "Do you think that David has released you to get Jenny's love?"

"That should be the reason, otherwise, why would they let me go?"

After remaining silent for a while, the poet said, "That means I lost my girlfriend because of you."

42

Jahangir, in an attempt to calm the poet, said, "No, maybe Jenny lied to save me."

The poet stared at Jahangir's eyes and replied in a cold voice, "Jenny never lies."

At this moment, there was no way to understand that there were two defeated people sitting face-to-face with a distance of miles between them. Jahangir had given up. But the poet was not a person to accept defeat so easily. His brain was working fast. On the day after Jahangir was caught, there was this headline on the newspaper, "Godfather Jahangir killed in an internal conflict: Police looking for the dead body in Kamrangir Char." There was a picture of Jahangir's real face beside the headline. The government did not get into the complications of the crossfire. There was a Bengali phrase, to kill the snake without breaking the stick. Its local English rhetoric could be termed as 'All are un-Official'. But Jahangir was supposed to die two more days later. David's people showed that paper to Jahangir jokingly. In that same news, there was the name of David as the new godfather, who was a personal favourite of the Home Minister Comrade Dastagir. The Home Minister picked up David from the leftist student organisation party in Jhenaidaha to the central committee. Before Comrade Dastagir became the Home Minister of the present coalition government, David had shown a great performance in every party showdown in Dhaka. He was also the main secret coordinator between the banned Sarbahara party and the clean image holder Comrade Dastagir.

David did not grow up through the extortion in slums and city corporation tender business like Jahangir or Kundu. Rather, the brave and stray politics that was created by the Communist Manifesto of Karl Marx and Frederick Engels had shaped his political mind setup. Comrade Dastagir took the full authority of underworld by taking Jahangir out of the picture at the right time and putting David in his place. The capitalist state could not run smoothly only under the visible administration; another invisible rule also ran parallel. This invisible rule was the main controller of the local and global channel of profiteering. One part of the American government had worked to combat Iraqi feudalism, and another part went there to earn billion dollars in the name of the development work. Profit could be found on both sides of the new capitalism—profit in war, and profit in peace. To keep control of these profits, there needs to be another rule by someone else; which is known by many names in different countries of the world: Mafia family, Underworld, Cosa Nostra, and Cartel. And its secret code name in Dhaka was 'Circle'.

Due to the downfall of Jahangir's monopoly power, the entire control of the Circle was now in the hands of comrade Dastagir through David. After listening to Jahangir, the poet Anindya Akash closed his eyes for some time. Then he opened his eyes and said to Jahangir, "Do you understand the similarity between us, Jahangir?"

Jahangir asked, "Where?"

"We are both defeated by David."

The poet remained silent for a while. Then he said, "And do you know where the difference is?"

"Where?"

"You've accepted your defeat, but I won't. You have lost your empire, and I have lost my empress. Most probably, David has impressed Jennifer. I won't get her back until she comes out of that trance. Comrade Dastagir is the main source of power for David. He is powerful only as long as Dastagir remains powerful. You should start to get back to your business slowly."

Jahangir lowered his head. "No. Everyone knows that I am dead. A person who is declared dead by the media does not get heaven or hell."

"That's even more helpful for you! You can get everything in order without any problem now."

"No, that's not possible for me anymore."

"Which means you will have to live the remaining part of your life miserably, by pulling rickshaw…haha! But you can't even do that, Jahangir."

Do you know why? Because local thugs will come to you and joke with you…"Hey Jangia, heard that you were such a big don…" ha ha!

Jahangir, holding down the hand of the poet, and eyes turned red with insult, said, "If you say one more thing, I will bury you on the ground."

Jahangir was back in his own self. Poet Anindya Akash was waiting to see this. Now he said with a compromising and friendly voice,

"You're not finished, Jahangir. Start again from scratch, you know where to start that from and how to start. The power is like a drop of honey among a group of hungry ants. Everybody wants to put a tongue there at any price. You can never befriend with someone with a greedy heart. The power is always surrounded by greedy ants, hostile enemies in the guise of friends. Let me teach you a trick, Jahangir. Before you look at people, look at their character. You'll get everything there – tigers, hyenas, wolves, foxes, snakes, crocodiles, and everything else according to your choice that you need for the war. Maybe you'll even get one or two humans there, too. Use them according to their character. The good news for you is that you'll find these animals abundantly. And the bad news is, David's probably got a genuine human beside him already. And if David finds this out, or if he recognises Jenny's power, then our job will become tough. But there is also an advantage."

Jahangir wanted to know, "What advantage?"

"Jenny will unknowingly bring David to us…"

The poet stared at Jahangir without finishing the sentence. Jahangir's eyes started to glow with the light of hope.

# Chapter 9

David's car was mixed in the crowd of thousands of cars moving towards Dhaka. Three phones were continuously ringing.

Johnny was driving the zip, and David was sitting beside him in the front seat. Aslam was sitting in the middle of the backseat, and Jenny and Kibria were on both sides. Some of the wards of Dhaka who had not yet entered the Circle had already made a phone call and pledged their loyalty. And those who were left were still hesitant. They were Jahangir's trusted people, working with him from long ago. But they knew very well that they could not survive outside the Circle in any way.

A group of mysterious people were coming forward from different parts of Dhaka to Motijheel. Most of them never went public. They were coming to welcome the new Circle boss in Motijheel's Janata Tower.

The clever people always create a good name to do something evil beforehand. One such name was 'Janata Tower'. During the war of liberation, Motijheel, Nawabpur and Islampur were controlled by Bihari Nowshad. Nowshad was a member of Ayub Khan's student organisation named National Student Federation, or briefly called NSF, and he used to terrorise the Dhaka city under the control of Panch Pattu's group. During the war, Nowshad had the responsibility of looting and spying from under the direct supervision of Pakistan army brigadier Baluch Arbaz. The seven-storied building Azadi Tower was used to store the looted money and gold at that time.

Baluch Arbaz could not understand that the direction of war would turn in such short notice. He stored a lot of money and almost ten tons of gold, to transfer in the first opportunity to West Pakistan. But no one could anticipate the fall of Dhaka so suddenly. Bihari Nowshad and his team died in the hands of the freedom fighters. The Indian army came and captured Azadi Tower. By then, there was no sign of gold or money. The stories of money and gold spread like wildfire. After the departure of the Indian Army, several groups of freedom fighters of Dhaka had fought between themselves to capture Azadi Tower. Later it was turned into a temporary camp for the Rakkhi Bahini, or the National Security Force (NSF). After that, the ownership of the Azadi Tower has been changed every time the government has been changed. The name changed into Janata Tower from Azadi or Independence Tower.

However, the tower's character remained the same. The present identity of the 18-storey Janata Tower was hidden behind the signboard of a small co-operative bank. There was a big vault beside the little vault of the bank, and the money from extortion, bribe, corruption, tender, land grab, contract killings, and even a part of the hijacking that happened every day in Dhaka city was stored in that big vault through different stages. The Circle boss had a secret and official codename – Accountant. The Accountant kept all the accounts of that money. Basically, most of this money was spent in national elections and in party activities. The Circle boss ran everything like a shadow government sitting at the top floor of Janata Tower. Jahangir was the accountant so far, and from today it was David. Surprisingly, no news of this mysterious tower ever went to the media. The general public never got to know why sometimes there was no electric power from 12 to 3 am without any apparent reason around the Janata Tower. In that darkness, some cars with the national flag came to a stop in front of the building, and the passengers in those cars had very familiar faces, that no one recognised only because of the darkness.

After these two words from Aslam, all phones became silent. A thin smile was playing in David's face, which disappeared after just a moment. Jennifer was sitting in the back seat of the car, from where she could have the view of a side of David's face. She had seen that smile. She could not understand, however, how the four men in the car kept themselves so calm even after being with such an attractive woman as herself. But she could realise this much that these people were immersed in the most important work of their life. There was an uncomfortable silence inside the car. Jennifer could feel that the men around her were tense about something. A message alert sound suddenly broke that silence. Jennifer let out a breath. Aslam read the message, "Sikandar of Gupibag has reached with his people."

David asked, "Is that good news or bad?"

"I think its good news."

David thought for a few moments, then said, "He cannot be trusted, keep an eye on him."

"Okay. I'll tell Haris from Gabtoli to do that."

"Good."

The car was going towards Dhaka, but now through an unknown route. It left the main road. The traffic on this road was very low. Grey darkness on the fields of trees surrounded the green fields on both sides of the road. Maybe they were using some alternative way to hide themselves. Through the village's lonely darkness, a group of 12 cars was moving forward, silently like ghosts.

David kept his eyes on the road. Control of the city might look easy until now, but he could not be absolutely sure. He was going to jump inside a room full of deadly snakes. At any moment, someone may strike him. The most foolish thing in this terrible game was that everyone depended on courage and strength. He knew that if he had to win in this game, he would have to depend on technique and intelligence. He needed to be calm. Jennifer also thought similarly. How did this man keep himself so cool in such a complex time?

Jennifer was in danger until she knew what David planned to do with her. But the excitement of being in a strange situation was also equal. It felt like she was also a part of it. She prayed for David's success because he refrained from doing a major job, only because of her words. A person who responded to the truth from a hostile environment was surely different from others. Suddenly, the car stopped. Jennifer looked outside the window and recognised the place. Bashundhara Residential area on the left side of the road and Purbachal highway to the right. Her flat was just five minutes' walk from here. But how did they know that! She did not know that David did a thorough search using her phone number about her. Every information, including her ID, was found correct. David made everything sure about her. Before Jennifer could say anything, he turned and said, "If you have so many cars in front of your flat, everyone could become alert. So I stopped a little further." Aslam returned Jennifer's phone back.

Jennifer opened the door on the right and went to David's side. She kept wondering what to say for a moment, then said, "Thank you for the lift."

David looked at with a slight smile that vanished in a second. Then he said to Johnny, 'move'.

David's car disappeared quickly. All the other cars followed him. Suddenly a deep silence came from all four sides. Jennifer did not know what would happen to these people after a while. There was a fear for David in her. She looked at her watch and saw that it was 1.45 in the night.

# Chapter 10

Motijheel
2:15 at night.

In the darkness of load shedding, the tall skyscrapers were looking like a ghost.

The office area generally remained solitary in the night. And there was no moon tonight, the sky covered with deep black clouds. It was raining somewhere far away, the scent of rain coming down in the air. The petrol cars of Motijheel Police Station did not seem to be in any hurry to start the second shift. There were four turns in the 300 square meter area surrounding Janata Tower. In every turn, two or three zip cars or microbuses waited. At first, it would seem that the cars had been parked for the night there. But a group of armed people was sitting in those vehicles in total darkness. Although all of them were working for David, some of them were forced to take his side. And forcing someone might be very dangerous because they would change their loyalty as soon as they saw any resistance from Jahangir.

About seventy to eighty people were sitting and standing on the street in front of Janata tower. They were spread in small groups of three to four people, all silent. Nobody uttered a word except emergency. The phones were all silent or in vibration mode, their alight screens looking like fireflies in the darkness.

The first three cars from David's team appeared in front of Janata Tower.

Some men got down in a silent but quick way from the cars, like silhouettes. They were with Tunda Mirza of Savar, and David's main strength. They came and took control of the main entrance of Janata Tower and its surroundings. Now

David's car arrived, and the remaining eight cars followed him. Everyone got down from their vehicles and created a protective barrier around David's car.

Aslam came down first, then Johnny and Kibria. David got down after them. Mirza came to him and said in his ear, "Everything is all right, brother."

This moment was the most dangerous. Anything could happen in the dark. There might be a sniper sitting in one of the dark rooftops with a night vision telescope, waiting to press the trigger. So, Aslam, Johnny and Kibria surrounded David by forming a close circle. And in another circle, Mirza's 20 armed men surrounded them. There was no sound except the Janata Tower's own generator droning away. The effect of cold air was increasing, rain would probably start at any second. David looked at the sky for a moment, then turned his eyes towards the 18th floor. It seemed that in this office area of Motijheel, the lights were on in just one floor of one building.

Home Minister Comrade Dastagir himself welcomed David in front of the 18th-floor elevator. He embraced David after shaking hands with him. "Comrade, my Comrade. Congratulation."

He put a hand on his shoulder and almost dragged him to the 18th floor's co-operative bank conference room. Ten people, including the five heads of the pentagon, also entered with David. The influential commissioners of different wards of Dhaka, four MPs, and some of the controversial police officers in white clothes were already waiting for him there. Owners of 10 contracting companies were also among them. Two prominent leaders of the labour union, General Secretary of Transport Owners Association, some former student leaders of the government and the opposition, and two well-known media moguls could be seen there too. There were no seating arrangements in the conference room. Everyone was standing. Comrade Dastagir dragged David forward to stand in front of everyone, then like a proud father introducing his child, he said, "I want to introduce our new accountant, my most favourite comrade, David."

Dastagir remained silent for a while, watching for everyone's reaction. There was pin-drop silence across the whole room. This silence was saying something, and that is – we accept it.

Dastagir started again, "We have to have full authority and control in all areas of society for the welfare of the country and the people. That control is not possible for the government alone. Every country in the world has a shadow government along with the visible government. The stronger that shadow government is, the more powerful the visible government will be. The basis of the capitalist state is a benefit. The bonds become tough when one person is benefited by the other. And these bonds form national ties, national solidarity. Surely I have made my point clear." Comrade Dastagir smiled. Then he looked at David and said,

"Circle has got a good accountant this time. I have known David for a long time, from field politics. By the knowledge of his courage and calculation, the country will surely benefit." Comrade Dastagir laughed once more.

Dastagir introduced David, the new underworld boss of Dhaka while discrediting capitalism in an official language as much as possible. Everyone came forward and started to shake hands. In the end, suddenly Kushtia's Kana Faruk came to stand in front of him. As soon as David saw him, Faruk grabbed his hand tightly. David took a few moments to recognise him. As soon as he recognised the man, David wanted to take out his pistol. Kana Faruk anticipated that, so he got hold of his hand before that. Slowly David turned to look at Comrade Dastagir, who was watching him so far. As soon as their eyes met, Dastagir nodded to reassure him about Faruk.

Fifteen years ago, Comrade Bimal Das, the most honest and dedicated leader of the Communist Party was publicly shot dead in Paltan. The most vocal protest against that murder was Bimal's friend and co-worker Dastagir. Bimal Das was young David's political guru and ideal. He taught David many the complex principles of Leninism, Marxism etc. in a very simple manner. David could not have accepted that death even today. No trial had been staged about the killing of comrade Bimal. If Bimal Das survived, then Dastagir could never have got the party's top post, and he could not become a minister by means of Bourgeois politics either. Kana Faruk took part in murder and robbery as a business under the control of a misguided faction of Communist Party named 'Sarbahara' or proletariat. He was a top terrorist in Kushtia, Jhenaidah, Jessore and Khulna region. Many people of the party knew that Kana Faruk was brought to Dhaka to murder Comrade Bimal Das. But David understood only today who had brought him.

Despite being a part of the capitalist bourgeois politics, Dastagir's style was to publicly condemn this type of politics continuously. This style gave him a type of clear-cut image. Each of these so-called clarities was taken as fun by everyone. It is a tragedy that the existence of Comrade Dastagir's socialist dream survived only in the midst of this fun.

"The good bourgeois want to use the communists to keep the bad bourgeois under control. Let them wait a few days, then they will know their ends," said Comrade Dastagir, in a very loud voice, while keeping a hand on the shoulder of MP Adu Bhuiyan. Adu had the sole control of the drug trade in the Hill tracts of Bangladesh including Cox's Bazar.

Everyone surrounding him started to laugh. Adu Bhuiyan's potbelly started to tremble with his booming laugh. David could feel without looking that Faruk was looking at him intently from a corner of the crowd. Falsehood, treachery and betrayal were common in the world where David lived. But this new face of Dastagir that he saw today-he still could not believe it. When Dastagir put his hand on David's shoulder, it really felt like a father's hand. But that hand could push him down into a deep pit at any moment. This thought created helplessness inside him, and he made a grim determination – Bimal Das's death must be avenged. Just at that moment, he remembered the girl. What was she saying – there was only one difference between humans and monsters. Humans could forgive, but monsters couldn't. David suddenly realised that he did not ask her name.

# Chapter 11

"You're not writing anything lately."

"How can I write when I get to see you so rarely these days?"

"I'm never far from you!"

"Yes, but I cannot find you."

"That's precisely your problem, poet. I'm here, but you cannot find me. Did you lose me?"

Jenny asked the question and then sat staring at poet Anindya Akash, a mischievous smile playing in her lips.

The poets also laughed and said, "Everyone is careful about expensive things so that they don't have to lose them."

"You're right. We generally don't lose expensive things, but the problem is that the precious things are often stolen or robbed. You need power and courage to protect it."

"Love is the source of that strength and courage."

"The love you are talking about – its main foundation is faith. The love you write about in your poems."

"Am I different from my poems?"

"You yourself have written:

Before reading poetry, Read the poet.

"The more I read you, the more I'm moving away from you. Again, when I reread your poem, I come back to you like an enchanted person. What is this strange game of coming closer and moving away from that I am stuck in, poet? It seems that I've to stop either reading you or your poetry. Tell me, poet. Which one do I stop?"

Jenny stared at the poet's face with questions in her eyes.

The poet could not find anything to say in answer. So Jenny saved him from answering and said, "I really need a cup of coffee now. Would you take one too? Oh, first tell me why didn't you have lunch today? It's almost 5 pm now, but you didn't eat anything yet!" Anindya Akash was at a loss to answer again, but his mind was filled up with love for this girl. No one in this city asked him this question with so much affection and care. It was true that he did not eat anything today. How did Jenny understand that? She went to University cafeteria to bring some food. She ordered a lot of food and picked them up on a tray. A woman's care for a hungry man is a heavenly scene. No poem could express that beauty. The poet stared at the woman returning with food.

As soon as the poet saw the food, he understood how much hungry he was. He did not get any taste from eating with the spoon, so he started to plunge his hand into the Biriyani. But just then, Jenny caught his hand and said, "Go to the washroom and wash your hands well before eating."

The poet looked at her eyes and said, "But then the touch of your hand will be washed!"

Feeling shy, Jenny let his hand go. The poet started eating with a spoon. Jenny looked at her wristwatch and said, "My classes will start soon after. That's the last class, do you want to wait or not?"

"Can't I be a student in your class?"

Jenny laughed and said, "No."

"Then I'll wait. If you come after a hundred years, you will see that I'm waiting for you here, and eating Biriyani." The poet always fascinated Jenny with all these words. She arranged her things in the bag and stood up, pulling a lock of his hair playfully before going away.

The poet closed his eyes and inhaled deeply. Jenny was leaving, but she was leaving a strange perfume in North South University's cafeteria.

# Chapter 12

Even without counting the other sources, an amount of almost a thousand crore taka was collected annually from the footpath of Dhaka.

As soon as the government changed, the control of footpaths, bus-stands, cattle markets, mass markets, cable line business of different areas, drug business, garments business etc. was changed from hand to hand. Nothing in this town was done for free. The people who slept in the footpath, who pulled rickshaws, they all had to pay their share. Prostitutes in the streets also had to pay. Van puller or eggs, nuts and fruits vendors had to pay fifty to three hundred takas every day. Those who collected this money were called Linemen and Foot leaders. The Linemen collected the money and handed over to the local party men. That party man would then send the money to the ward commissioner or the representative appointed by him. The ward commissioner kept one part of the money for himself, sent another portion to the local police station, and the rest to Janata Tower. This private tax system had been standing on a very strong system since the Pakistan period. The main power of this system's engine was 'Terror'. And to create this panic one needed a person like Subrata, Jahangir or David. Media promoted their atrocities; gave them the title 'Top Terrorist' and the system secretly called them 'Accountants'. David knew that from the top of the 18th floor, the empire he was given had a really hard surface below. He had been raised to this height so that he could easily be thrown down after his purpose had ended.

The whole horizon of the sky could be seen from the top floor glassed office Janata Tower. A flying buzzard roamed around the sky, flying lazily in circles. It was a Bhuban Cheel,

David could recognise from the white patches on its chest. The bird was flying alone in the sky and seemed to be looking at David. David was just as alone as that bird, though he was now the city's undeclared emperor. Four months had passed since he had been the master of this three thousand square feet office at the top floor of Janata Tower. There were about 80 armed men spread across the whole tower. The whole city was now under his control. For the maximum period of the day, David just stared at the city from the other side of the glass panel. So many things were happening every moment inside that city that could not be seen from here through the glass. But every event that happens is tied together in a big thread. Tugging a small string from that thread could break the foundations of many big mountains. This thread was called the system.

David's job was to run the dark part of the system. But he did not want this. Against the capitalist exploitation and the economic inequality of humanity, socialism felt like the light of freedom to him. From the first year of college, he joined the movement with a view to change the time and people's life. But the deeper he entered, the more deeply he saw the frustration, and division within the leaders. After the fall of socialist countries, the frustration and split increased further. In socialist Russia, those who thought that being freed from the iron rule of Lenin, Stalin, and Khrushchev meant freedom, they deemed after some days that independence meant nothing but being wealthy. Likewise, some persons with broken dreams in this country started killing and robbery in the name of finishing off enemies of the people. They gave slogans like *'Joy Sarbahara'* or *'Hail to the proletariat'* when they returned from those robbing and killing missions. Being involved in that proletarian politics, and by successful operations of murders and other atrocities one after another, David was marked as an asset by the leaders of the party's high command. By then, the high command had involved themselves in the sharing of power of capitalist politics. David did not have any way to go back because of the numerous robberies and murder cases. He also wanted to see the end of it. Perhaps this 18th floor was the highest point of rising for him. Comrade David was now the custodian of bourgeois extortion and robbery.

"Boss."

Aslam's call breaks David's flow of thoughts, who was looking at the distance through the glass window.

David left a sigh and turned around. Aslam asked, "What to do with Jinjira's Liton?" He looked down at the floor without looking at David. David knew what Aslam actually wanted to hear.

To Aslam, the easiest solution to the problem was to 'kill'. It was easy for him to solve the problem once and for all by killing rather than facing a problem on a regular basis.

But David had another plan.

"Let's see what we can do."

Aslam came out behind David. There were more than ten people, including Johnny and Kibria in the outer lobby, who always remained with David. They were all tested for a long time ago. David had picked them up from different places. Four of them had been released from jail. They arrived behind a packaging factory at an abandoned warehouse in the Tejgaon industrial area. Liton was held here.

Liton had worked for Jahangir for a very long time. He expelled David's men from Jinjira. Local leader Ishtiaq was giving him shelter secretly. Ishtiaq worked for the opposition lobby of Dastagir. Jinjira was the first station in Dhaka for trafficking drugs through water transport. Whoever controlled Jinjira, controlled the drug business of Dhaka. Liton had been beaten a lot after being caught. He gave up hope of his life. He was tied to a chair now. Another chair was brought in front of him. David sat there, and the rest stood around them. Liton had heard David's name before, but this was the first time he saw him face-to-face. He could understand that his time was over. He just stared blankly at David. David looked at him for a while, then said, "I don't have any value for dead bodies. Tomorrow your dead body will burn to ashes in the brick kiln."

Liton's eyes became full of tears. He said in a dry voice, "Brother, I have a motherless son. If you give me my life back, I will leave this city with my son; you will never see me again."

"I'm making the arrangements for you to leave this world, not only Dhaka."

"Brother, my son will die then."

"You didn't think of the future of your son before. If you did, then you wouldn't have picked a fight with me."

"I made a mistake, brother."

"Do you want to correct that mistake?"

"Yes, brother. Give me a chance for the sake of my son."

"You'll betray again if you're given the opportunity."

"I'll be your slave for the rest of my life, and I'll live only for my son. Please forgive me, brother."

David looked at everyone's team and said, "Can he be forgiven?"

Everyone said in unison, "No boss, he can't be. You cannot find a second treacherous pig like him in the whole of Jinjira."

Liton's hope of survival was shattered at that moment.

David remained silent for a moment, then said, "If I pardon you in front of all these people, can you prove them false? Can you?"

Lipton said in the middle of crying, "Of course, brother."

David looked at his eyes and tried to read them, but Liton's eyes were obscured by his tears. A tear was an expression that had many hidden meanings. David tried to read them all. The problem was, Liton was not crying to save his own life, he was crying for his son. David could understand that.

"Go. You're free."

Immediately, Aslam and some of the others started to protest, 'Boss…'

David did not let them talk any longer. He told Liton, "Everything will remain the same way that you so long for. There will be no change. What you had done for Jahangir, now you will do it for me and keep my men with you." He gestured to one of the guys to open his bindings. The man did it. Liton could not believe his eyes. This was not the rule at this line. People were killed because of trivial reasons. Leaving the opponent alive after having him in such a weak position was not only surprising, but unbelievable, and it was being done by none other than a terrible murderer like David. Liton just stared blankly at David's face. He did not know what to say. David said, "The opportunity is but one. Just remember that if you betray me, I'll kill your son in front of your eyes, then I'll kill you."

David did not give Liton any chance to express his emotions or gratitude. He left the place and told Johnny on the way, "Make arrangements so that Liton can reach safely to his area."

On the way to the car, not many were with David. Aslam used this chance to ask, "Boss, what has happened to you? If you keep on forgiving this way, then everyone will start to think you weak."

Before he opened the door of the car, David said, "The opposite can be true, also. It takes power to forgive someone. Forgiveness is a virtue of the powerful."

These doctrines did not enter Aslam's head. But to him, his boss David seemed to be someone extraordinary. His feeling towards David could be described as respect mixed with extreme fear. Suddenly Aslam remembered something. He said lightly, "I heard something similar from someone else before, boss."

Johnny had started the car and was already moving. David kept his eyes locked on the road and ordered Aslam, "Find her."

# Chapter 13

"I'm film director Alam Sufian, from Dhaka. How are you, Shaheed Bhai?"

There was no response from the other side.

"Hello, can you hear me?"

This time the answer came, although after a few moments of silence. "What do you want?"

"We're going to make a movie that will require your cooperation."

Then the phone line was disconnected. Two more attempts were made, but he did not receive the call that day.

A week later, Alam Sufian called again and came to the point without any further ado. He said, "Shaheed Bhai, we want to make a movie about the life of Imdu from Kaliganj. We've come to know that you used to do politics with him. So we need your cooperation." This was not new, because he gave some interviews in the media after the death penalty of Imdu was carried out. But that was a long time ago. Shaheed Chairman started responding to the telephone after this and answered one or two questions about Imdu. After almost a month later the film director coaxed Shaheed Chairman to sit in an interview with him. Sitting beside the big pond of the old muslin cotton mill of Upazila Sadar, Shaheed Chairman talked about many things. Alam Sufyan kept writing notes on the parts he deemed necessary.

Imdadul Haq Imdu was the son of a farmer named Ashraf Ali, and he was born in the village Satani Para in Kaliganj. He studied in Khaykora High School until class seven. After independence, he emerged in the field of politics by the hands of Ali Hossain Talukdar, a leader of JSD Kaliganj district. Later, there started a conflict between him and Ali Hossain about the sharing of robbed goods and money. The local JSD was divided into two parts from this conflict. Not only was the political party divided, even Kaliganj itself parted into two hostile factions. There was a railway that ran through the town. The south side of the railway line was occupied by Ali Hossain, and the north side was occupied by Imdu. They started making their own bases and bunkers in the same way the security barriers were made by using sandbags in time of war, and killed each other. Shaheed Chairman, while talking about those days, had a dazed expression in his face, as if he was back at that time again. The thought that his stories will come alive in the movie gave Shaheed Chairman a new pleasure. The director Alam Sufian took leave for that day, saying that he would come back next week to finalise the shooting location. Previously, Shaheed Chairman had brought two people along with him. They waited for him far away. But on the day of finalisation, Shaheed Chairman came alone. He had made a warm friendship with the film director, Alam. From the afternoon, the director and the chairman set two or three places for shooting. By the evening they crossed the Silo or food storage near Shitalakshya and started to walk by the river. There was an old Kali temple here, made during the period of Raja Rajendra Narayan. Though there was nothing but a wreck of ruins now, yet Kali worship still went on there. Situated in the scenic landscape of the Shitalakshya River, the temple created a mysterious atmosphere. No people came here once darkness fell. The director said that he was looking for a place just like this to shoot an important part of the story. The darkness started to become heavier as he started to note the technical aspects of camera angles and short divisions etc. The early winter air coming from the river was filling the environment with a strange feeling. A broken row of stairs from the temple went down to the river. There was a tall pillar standing there.

Sitting down there, and listening about Imdu's terrible acts, Alam Sufian took out the flask of tea from his bag and used the lid as a cup to pour some of the fresh tea brought from Kaliganj Bajar. He gave the cup to Shaheed Chairman.

The smell of tea was really refreshing. Alam Sufian took out a packet of biscuits from his bag and gave some to Shaheed Chairman, and took one himself. Immersed in the story, Shaheed Chairman sipped his tea and bit the biscuits as well. There was only one cup, so one had to wait for the other to finish drinking. So Alam Sufian was listening to the story and waiting for the mug to be empty. Shaheed Chairman became silent after having the last sip of tea. No sound could be heard except the crickets. Film director Alam Sufian's voice broke the silence. "Shaheed Bhai, do you know that Jahangir has survived?"

Shaheed Chairman looked in the darkness with equally dark eyes and asked quietly,

"What was mixed in that tea?"

"Don't worry, Shaheed Bhai. That's not poison, you won't die."

"What do you want?"

"I do not want anything, Shaheed Bhai. Whatever he wants, he will tell you himself. Jahangir was waiting nearby, now he came out of the dark and stood face to face with Shaheed."

He said in a very easy voice, "You have to work for me, Shaheed."

The drug that was mixed with tea was called 'Kratom'. It made the body unconscious while keeping the brain active.

Shaheed's eyes were full of wonder and surprise. He muttered to himself,

"David has not only broken the rule, but he also made it totally void. But this is so foolish of him."

Now the Chairman said, "You've died, Jahangir. Who works for the dead?"

"You'll work to make me alive again."

"David did precisely that."

"No, David saved me from dying once, only to die every hour, every day. I won't live like this. Save me. Work for me. I will take back Dhaka."

Shaheed Chairman could not move at all. He was looking at Jahangir with anger and surprise. Jahangir lit a cigarette. He had a piece of cloth, perhaps a towel wrapped in his neck like a muffler, and wearing a Lungi. There is no way to understand that it was Jahangir.

"Come to the system," he said.

"It'll take a long time to come to the system. I don't have that time at this moment. And I don't need the full five points, you just manage Joynal, maker of Tongi. Joynal is your own man."

Shaheed Chairman said in a hard voice, "I have kissed David's hand."

"You will kiss my hand in a few days."

"Come to the system."

"Shake hand with me."

"I kissed David's hand."

Jahangir understood what the meaning of this was. This was the reason Shaheed Chairman was regarded in the underworld Circle as a person of honour and respect. Even if the whole world turned to the other way, his words and actions would not change in any way. Shaheed Chairman was an essential character in both of the first and last scene in the drama of Dhaka Circle. Jahangir did not want to do the job that he had to do now. But there was no way out. Taking a last puff of smoke, he flicked the cigarette away from his hand, then took the towel from his neck. He tied two knots at two ends of the cloth. The Chairman saw his careful work. It was the method of Thuggees, a very old style. Nowadays, nobody used this method usually. Twenty-five years ago, Shaheed Chairman killed Anup, a contract killer and a widow mother's only son in this way, who worked for the Ali Hossain Group. When the mother came to take back her son's dead body, she said very calmly to the chairman, "You will also die like this."

But Jahangir was not supposed to know about that. Shaheed believed in karma. Perhaps his belief was going to turn into reality now.

After tying the knots, Jahangir tested them several times by pulling with strength. The drug's effect was now fully working on Shaheed Chairman's body. There was nothing that he can do but to stare helplessly. Slowly Jahangir stood up and came to stand behind the chairman. He wrapped the cloth in tight circles around the Chairman's neck. Just as he started to make his noose tighter, film director Alam Sufian alias poet Anindya Akash stopped him. "Wait, Jahangir. A poet does not have anything to do with a situation like this. I'd rather wait in front of the temple."

# Chapter 14

It had been around six months since that day. There was a slight change in rhythm in Jennifer's daily routine. She got absent-minded sometimes without any apparent reason. She checked her phone inbox frequently. The problem was that poet Anindya Akash could feel this change. He was also changing as the days passed. He had reduced the writing. Now he was always in a desperate and aggressive mood. Jenny could understand that there was no shortage of misconceptions in his love. But inside Jennifer, there was a wall. Even after trying a lot, she could not break that wall. She could not even understand why the wall was there and how it came to be. She only understood that the love of the poet was authentic. But she still could not reach the same conclusions about the human Akash. A man who had a difference between his beliefs and actions would be revealed inevitably at the end of the day. The more the poet expressed himself, the harder Jenny's wall was becoming. Sometimes the poet vanished somewhere and again came back to the cafeteria of her university, waiting for her all day long. Jenny liked the poet's company and his boyishness.

"Hey, are you feeling sad?"

"Yes, I am."

"Hmm, I think you're caught in a Monkey Trap."

"What is that?"

"You're stuck in a trap that is used to catch monkeys."

"What do you mean?"

"Have you ever seen any such trap?"

"No, I haven't."

"Then listen. A box or hole is used to catch monkeys. The mouth of that box or hole is made in such a way that a monkey can easily reach inside the mouth. The hunter puts some food inside the hole or box. The monkey can easily put his hand inside, but when he tries to pull out the food, his hand becomes too big. Now if the monkey leaves the food inside, then he can bring his hand out. But he's so greedy, so he doesn't loosen his fist. He just tries to get away with the food. As usual, a hunter comes and kills him.

Moral of the story is, we try to keep our pains away while clutching them in our hands. Only when we loosen our hand, we can get rid of it. The main reason behind all our hardships is holding up things. Leave it and be free like a bird. You won't be upset again."

"Does it mean that those who are living in pain are all trapped monkeys?"

Jennifer started to laugh after hearing this. After some time, she said, "Yes, greed makes a man a monkey until he is killed by a hunter." Poet Anindya Akash became silent. He could understand what she meant by that. Before going out of the cafeteria, he said to Jenny, "You all live as the purest humans. Let me die as a monkey."

Jennifer was startled to see Aslam.

When the peon came to the teacher's room and said that there was someone to meet her, Jenny was a little surprised. The poet never asked for her this way. He came to the cafeteria, sat in his specific corner and gave her a text. Still, she thought maybe it was the poet. She tried to compose herself quickly. Her students were watching her from the background. Aslam's dress-up was completely incompatible with the surroundings.

"Remember me?"

"Yes. But why are you here?"

"I could call you, but you would have been in trouble then. Your phone is bugged. So I directly came here."

"Every phone in this country is bugged, that's nothing new. But what do you want from me?"

"Boss David wants to meet you."

"Why does he want to meet me? And why I should meet him?"

"You can hear from the boss why he wants to see you. And if you don't want to go, then it's fine."

Aslam took out an address from his pocket and handed it to Jennifer. As soon as she opened it, he started to walk in the opposite direction. The paper had a restaurant address, date and time. Without any second thought, Jenny decided to go.

The date was Monday, at 6 pm. She took a day's leave at the university. She was really excited, because that day she saw the start of a big event but did not know what would happen after that. Today she was going to know it all. There is a strange reaction inside Jenny which shook her inside. She did not understand why, but she was shaking inside. But it was not fear. It was nothing like the fear that should come from meeting a gangster-like David. Today it seemed that she might have been waiting for this day for the last six months. The name of the restaurant was 'Sky Home', on 12th floor in Banani's Kamal Ataturk Avenue.

When she reached there, a sudden thought came to her. She did not say anything about whether she would meet David. Besides, she behaved roughly with Aslam. Now, what if David does not come?

Two young men in security guards uniform approached as she went for the lift. One of them asked, "Madam, may I know your name?"

"Why?"

"Excuse me, but today we have a special guest. I just want to check if you are that person."

Embarrassed, Jenny could not think of what to say. Then she almost blurted, "I am Jennifer Ahmed Jenny."

They went rigid as soon as they heard the name. Opening the lift door with an elaborate gesture, the first talked in the walkie-talkie, "*Guest is here.*" The guards remained behind. Another guard entered the lift with Jenny.

The lift stopped on the 12th floor. Three men in similar restaurant dress welcomed her. Jenny took this reception normally. This was normal for most restaurants.

One introduced himself in a gentle voice as the restaurant manager. But she had to pause once entering inside because the whole restaurant was empty. The manager took her to the restaurant's special corner to a reserved table. Jenny understood the reason for the restaurant's name now. The corner had been arranged in such a way that it really felt like a house in the sky. But why was the restaurant empty? Did she arrive before the restaurant opened? Looking at the phone's clock, she saw that it was now three minutes to six. She wanted to ask the manager, but the manager was nowhere to be seen. At this moment, Jennifer was sitting alone in a huge restaurant of about four thousand square feet. Classical piano music was playing in the sound system. After five minutes, the manager returned with a fruit bucket and fresh orange juice. Two waitresses were accompanying him. The manager served the food in his own hand, and the girls helped him. Jenny worriedly asked, "Did I come before the restaurant was opened?"

The manager bowed before her respectfully and said, "No, ma'am. Our restaurant opens at 4 pm. You came at the right time."

"Then why is no one else here?"

"Ma'am, an important person, has booked our entire restaurant today. You are his guest."

Jennifer thought, then surely more guests will come.

As if sensing this thought, the manager said, "You are the only guest in our guest list today. We are always around you. Whatever you need, just call for us."

They left. The girls stayed close so that they could respond to her at any moment. Jenny understood the whole thing now. David actually booked the entire restaurant today to meet with her only. A mixed emotion started to build up inside her. Why is David paying her so much attention suddenly? And what if she refused to come today? How embarrassing would it have been? When she was thinking about all these, Kibria entered the restaurant, accompanied by ten others. They all sat in the distant tables. Kibria approached her.

"Do you recognise me?"

Jenny smiled. "Yes."

"You have to wait a little bit. Boss is almost here."

"No problem."

All the people sitting inside the restaurant now were David's men. They were whispering between themselves, so even if there were ten to twelve people here, it was still almost silent as it was before. After more than fifteen minutes later, David entered the restaurant with Aslam and ten other people in the restaurant. His companions scattered throughout the entire restaurant and took the position. There were twenty-five armed men in the restaurant now. David went straight to the corner where Jenny was sitting. There was a lot of difference between the person whom Jenny met that day, and the man she saw today, who was wearing a white shirt with blue denim, and an ash-coloured blazer on top. With this attire and crew-cut hairstyle, David looked like more like a football coach than a gangster. But as soon as she looked at his eyes, she identified them to be the same pair of eyes that she saw on the first day. David sat down in front of her and said, "Sorry for being late."

"It's okay," Jenny replied with a smile. "Actually, I am here to know what else happened that day."

"I've called you here to tell you about these things precisely."

Jenny was surprised, "Really?"

David nodded and said, "I am really being benefitted by applying your theory."

Jenny's eyes became wide with excitement. "Seriously!"

"Yes," replied David. "And I'd like to inform you that I took control of Janata Tower without any problem that night."

"I couldn't sleep at that night."

"Why? Did I make you afraid?"

"No, it's not like that. Actually, I became a supporter of your team after spending several hours with you. My good wishes were with you," Jenny said with a smile.

David said, "You did a really big favour to me that day."

"How is that?"

"I've learnt something from you."

"What have you learnt?"

"I have learnt the trick to win my enemies without defeating them."

"Is it possible to win someone without defeating him first?"

"Yes, it is. Winning or losing is nothing but a feeling. You have to defeat your enemy in such a way so that he doesn't feel like he has lost. You have to bring him inside your grip, then offer him your friendship. Those who are defeated to me, I make them my friends. It has benefitted me because the unnecessary troubles are decreasing from my business now."

"Wow. Seems great."

"But I haven't told you about the real trick yet."

"What's that?"

"That trick is called forgiveness. I think that forgiveness is power."

Jenny jokingly said, "Interesting! A gangster has taken forgiveness as his trick to rule his kingdom. But you'll have to be weary in using this trick. Not everyone will understand the value of your forgiveness.2

"Anyone who doesn't will have to pay with his life."

Saying this, David became a little pensive. He tried to lighten the environment by saying, "Do we just keep on talking? Let's order the food." He gestured for the manager. The man seemed to be waiting for this moment because he appeared almost immediately. David told Jenny, "You are going to have an amazing menu for dinner tonight. But, first, tell me if you have any allergy in lobster?"

"No, I like lobster."

"That's great because they have a great lobster item here." David looked at the manager and said, "Oven-baked lobster with lemon and garlic butter."

Jenny suddenly realised that the restaurant was almost full of people now, and they were talking between themselves. But not a sound reached their table. The sound system was playing an unknown symphony of the piano. As the manager left with the order, Jenny said, "You must be enjoying your power."

David sipped his strawberry lemonade drink and said, "Power makes people lonely. How can you enjoy loneliness?"

"I do."

"Maybe you are talking about solitude, not loneliness."

"O my god! You are right, loneliness and solitude are two different things."

"You like solitude, and I'm lonely because of power."

Both started to laugh. Jenny said, "You look like a man who reads regularly."

"The type of politics that I was involved with, everyone had to study there."

"Are you talking about communism?"

David laughed out and said, "Yes, but I am a strayed communist. Didn't you see, I ordered bourgeois food just a few moments ago?"

"Where Russia and China are strayed, what can you do? But it's true that ideas don't die. Those who thought out communism, their target was to free people from capitalist oppression. Maybe the implementation had some flaws, so it failed in the last century. Some new generation in this century might remove those flaws to bring about a new version."

"I've learnt something in these days. An idea cannot be brought forward without an ideal man. A handful of people who strongly believe in something can change a state totally, so strong is the power of belief. You cannot be an ideal man by just reading theories. You have to stand against your own vices to become that. If the next generation can create such leadership, then your ideas have the chance to survive."

Jenny changed the topic and said, "You are always surrounded by these people. Why do you feel lonely, then?"

"None of them are my friends here. They just follow me. Well, not me actually, they follow my power. Some of them are ready to die for my power, too. Who is my friend then?"

"You never found a friend then?"

"There was only one man after my father, who I thought to be my friend. But just a few days ago I found out that he was responsible for the murder of his most intimate friend and comrade. I understood that real friendship is very rare, not everyone finds it."

The manager and waitresses served the food. Jenny asked between eating, "Why this call for a meeting suddenly?"

David stopped eating. After thinking for some moments, he said, "That day you said that if I become a forgiving person, you would love me. Just wanted to see if you were telling the truth."

Suddenly, Jenny felt so embarrassed and shy. Even David seemed to be on a loss of what to say. The music of the piano was playing, trying to break the awkward silence that originated between them.

At this moment, Aslam came and stood behind David. Jenny looked at him. David followed her gaze and turned. Aslam bowed low to say deliver news to him. Shaheed Chairman was murdered, probably by Jahangir.

# Chapter 15

After crossing the Buriganga River through Basila Bridge, the immediate area is Washpur. Jakir, the chief of the syndicate of Pickpockets, petty thieves and robbers and professional beggars in Dhaka lived and ruled in this area. Chota Jakir was the younger brother of the infamous pickpocket leader Kangali Mamun. The younger one came in charge when Mamun was killed in a crossfire with the Detective Branch. Jakir took the news of Jahangir's death with incredulity; he could not even believe it.

The night when Janata Tower was taken by David, Jakir and his group was ready to attack them at the first sign of a gang fight. But nothing happened, so they grudgingly surrendered to David's rule. Mamun and Jakir both came to their power in Jahangir's time. Whenever there was some trouble, they could safely shelter themselves in Jahangir's area, Keraniganj. Jakir did not forget those favours from Jahangir. So from the moment, he found Jahangir safe and sound, he dedicated himself in his service.

Washpur could still be called a village. Situated in the suburban Buriganga banks, it was an ideal place to work from all directions. Police were not very active here. Jakir had left his unfinished three-story building for Jahangir for the time being. The building was still not plastered, without any doors or windows. Two rooms on the first floor had been read for occupying within two days after Jahangir arrived. One of them was for the poet Anindya Akash. The second floor had the roof, but not any walls yet. There was no shortage of light and air here. The poet has brought a bed here for himself. Laying down here, he looked at the sky, the river, and felt the air in his body. Sometimes he wrote poetry. He smoked marijuana with Jahangir at night. The poet did not smoke cigarettes. He could not even tolerate the smoke of cigarettes. But staying with Jahangir had made him accustomed to marijuana. Jahangir stayed busy all day recreating his networks, and the poet helped him with suggestions. Already Anindya Akash had found out almost everything about the Dhaka underworld from Jahangir. The whole thing was like a game of chess to him. When he suggested something to Jahangir, he scratched plots and other necessary things on the ground. Sometimes Jahangir felt surprised at the poet's wit and clear conceptions, it seemed to him that the poet could reach for the presidential chair of America if he wanted. But the only thing he seemed to be interested in  was writing poems and running after girls.

At this moment the two of them were sitting silently on the third floor, facing the river. They had just finished two marijuana cigarettes.

The night's silence engulfed them. Two defeated men, eager to reach to their goals. But if someone saw them right now, he would not understand anything. One wanted the kingdom; another wanted the princess. But one thing was certain – the king had to die to fulfil their wish. The math might look simple outwardly, but there were some complex equations inside it.

Suddenly the poet broke the silence. "The king lives in a well-protected castle. There are two ways to kill him. One is, you will attack his castle with your troops. Break one side of the castle, then enter inside and kill the king. It's hard but possible."

The poet became silent again. Jahangir was waiting eagerly to know the second way. And the poet was trying out his patience. After about forty-five minutes of silence, Jahangir asked, "What's the second way?"

The poet replied after waiting twenty minutes more, "The King has put the main key of his castle in someone's hand. You can take that and get to the King without any fuss. This way is harder, but not impossible. If a man is born to design locks that are really hard to break, then another is also born with the intelligence to crack them. Nothing in this world is constant. So everything is possible. And if you gain that knowledge about 'possible' and 'possibility', then fifty per cent of your success is already achieved, because now you know that it's possible to win. Now you just have to play with the remaining fifty per cent."

"Then which way shall we follow?" Jahangir asked.

"Your defeat is hidden in your question, Jahangir Bhai."

"What do you mean?"

"By saying 'which way', you mean that you want to take one path among the two, and by doing that you are decreasing the fifty per cent chance of your winning. No, Jahangir Bhai. We won't do that. We'll take both ways."

The poet looked at Jahangir. His excitement and clear plan touched Jahangir too, and he smiled. The poet said, "Hey, Jahangir Bhai. You can smile too!"

Jahangir's grin widened. Anindya Akash said, "Heart feels suffocated when the brain works too much. My heart is losing love, Bhai. Please light another Shaltu, quickly."

Jahangir lit the third marijuana cigarette, took two puffs and handed it to the poet. Anindya Akash started to cough as soon as he inhaled the smoke. After a while, he said, "You have to have a love for everything, Jahangir Bhai. Without love, you cannot build an empire, and without love, you cannot destroy it."

The poet took another puff of smoke from the cigarette, held it inside his chest for several moments, and then let it go slowly. Then he gave the cigarette to Jahangir and said, "I'm not feeling very well these days. Tell your Jakir to bring two tribal girls from a massage parlour. But not Garo girls, they have really harsh hands. I need pure Chakma. Looks like Chinese people, but talks in pure Bengali."

Jahangir understood that the poet was completely high now.

# Chapter 16

Poet Anindya Akash was sitting as usual at the North-South university cafeteria. Jenny brought a tray with a lot of food for him, as she did every day. The poet felt really hungry whenever he came to meet Jenny. He never felt such hunger at any other moments. It was really strange. When the poet ate, Jenny looked at him with entranced eyes. She felt a deep affection for him. It seemed to her that the poet stored all his hunger just to eat in front of her. Jenny said, "thank you, Akash."

The poet stopped eating and said, "Why?"

"Because you have created the pair of eyes with which I see."

Akash resumed eating.

"I see this world with the eyes of your poetry. You have created them, so I thanked you. A human being needs some kind of philosophy to live. I have found it in your poems. You said that I was really brave that day. I found this courage because of your poems. That man, whom I saved, he also got his life back because of you. Your poems have given me the joy to live. I am in love with your poems, and your poems have made me love someone who is also created by your poems. I found him in your writings. I found the inner you inside David."

the poet refrained from expressing any thought. He just said, "I need a coffee now."

"You can finish your food; I will bring it."

Jenny went to fetch coffee. She did not know that a pair of eyes were looking at her. But there was no love there, they were the eyes of a murderer. When Jenny came back with the coffee, the poet kept eating attentively without looking at her.

He knew that if he looked at her eyes now, he could not conceal himself. But Jenny thought that he was feeling down.

So she asked, "Why are you sad, poet?"

The poet looked up after finishing his lunch. "I've taken my hand out of the trap. I won't be in pain anymore."

Jenny said happily, "that's the spirit."

"But there is a problem. A monkey who saved himself from the trap might turn dangerous."

"Why, poet? A man who breaks himself from the chains is a free man. Haven't you written…?"

"A free man does not need wine, woman or riches, Pointless desires."

"You've told everything, poet. I'm just translating."

The poet was feeling a storm of rage and fire was breaking everything inside him, but he did not let that come to his face. Smiling like an excellent actor, he said, "Congratulations, baby."

"Thank you, poet. You are an indispensable person to my love, and you will always be."

"I should celebrate this love of yours for David."

The poet started to rummage inside his bag and took out a parker pen. Giving it to Jenny, he said, "I've written a lot of your favourite poems with this pen. I want you to keep it always with you. No one else in this world is worthy of this pen."

Jenny felt really grateful, and her eyes started to fill up with tears. Holding the pen with both hands, she said, "From today, this is a special pen for me. I'll keep it with myself, but won't write anything except something really important. Thank you again, my poet." She put the pen in her bag.

Suddenly her mobile chimed a message tone. She read the massage, and said with a shy voice, "I've to go now, poet. David is waiting for me."

The poet said with a bright smile, "Of course. You must go now, go in love and ecstasy and don't forget to convey my greetings to him."

"I will, poet."

The poet was satisfied. He said, "I know that no one would be able to harm you. Still, these people are organised criminals, gangsters. So you should be weary."

"Don't worry at all. As long as I am with David, I feel like I am in the safest place in the world."

"If you say that, then it must be true. I'm relieved."

"I'm going now."

"Good luck, baby. And all the best."

Poet Anindya Akash looked for some time at the way she went. A sigh came out of his chest. Jenny disappeared on the curve of the long corridor. The poet sat down for a while with his eyes closed, then opened them again and started to do something very important.

The parker pen that he had given to Jenny, it was actually a voice-spying device. He could make it go live just by opening an app in his smartphone. The poet could easily hear the daily commotions of Bashundhara residential area as Jenny went through the roads. A car horn, rickshaw bells, hawkers shouting, and a cuckoo calling. The poet smiled. The cuckoo did not stop, calling continuously. Suddenly the poet wanted to know what month of the Bengali calendar was now.

# Chapter 17

Shaheed Chairman's death was taken as ominous news. Although the mainstream media did not regard it with importance, the underworld took it very seriously. To an ordinary person, Shaheed Chairman was nothing but an ordinary chairman of Kaliganj, but in the darkness, he was an important person of Dhaka circle. Whoever wanted to enter the circle, could not do it without Shaheed's blessings. He was an old witness who saw many changes inside the circle and remained present during many important events. The normal administration might look away from many events, but they all are watched by the underworld. The administrative net had many big holes, through which many important events might get slipped. But the circle did not work that way; it did not miss anything. When the police could not solve a murder case, snatching or other criminal activities, they took help from the circle. The circle helped the police in return for their own benefits. Almost all the robbery, snatching and contract killings were done by organised criminals. The police knew about their identities and whereabouts. They could find out a snatched moneybag from anywhere in Dhaka within an hour if they wanted. It was a common scene not only in Dhaka, but also in all big cities including New York, Paris, Havana, Mumbai, Bangkok etc.

The circle had found out that Jahangir was seen in Kaliganj before the day the murder happened. They understood that Jahangir had started his retaliation. It was an established rule that without killing the past boss, no new boss could rule the circle. But Jahangir was still alive, and he was trying to return to power. It became an open secret because of the murder of Shaheed Chairman. It was strange, but most of the circle members liked the fact that David did not murder Jahangir. He had become the most popular circle boss in history. Instead of brutal savagery that was common in the Dhaka underworld, David's forgiving nature had made him not only popular but also powerful. He was a safe shelter for many people without being a name of fear. This exceptional rise of David had broken many rules of the circle.

Murders and acts of revenge were common incidents previously, but now everyone came to David. He made judgments, and everyone obeyed him blindly.

Behind this remarkable rise of David was his application of human virtue, 'forgiveness' against cruelty, and extending the hand of friendship to the enemy. This sudden popularity of David's in the underworld had left comrade Dastagir in tension. In the past, all the people who went to Dastagir for solutions would now go to David. Underworld's control had long moved away from Dastagir's hand. Dastagir knew it, but the matter could not be brought publicly, because everyone still knew that David was his right hand. David also maintained his public loyalty to Dastagir. David had found a hard truth of underworld that everyone who had relied on power in this world had fallen rapidly and brutally. So he had started to depend on wit instead of power. The circle was a weapon for the politicians, but David had turned it into diplomacy. Dastagir had brought the murderer of comrade Bimal Das, Kana Faruk into daylight without feeling the need to consult with David. David had learnt about some big extortions by Kana Faruk, but he was ignoring them for now. He did not want to go into open conflict with Dastagir right now. He was waiting for a chance to avenge the murder of his favourite comrade, Bimal Das. No one knew that he was burning inside from the fire of retaliation.

# Chapter 18

The theory that worked behind this rise of David was named 'forgiveness'. Only two people knew that the person who taught David this theory was named Jennifer Ahmed Jenny, a woman with a tremendous personality. Those two people were David and poet Anindya Akash. This was the first time a woman entered his life who brought the feeling of love for him. David was not accustomed to this feeling before. His life of thirty-seven years had been spent mostly in Jail, crossing the border to India, being a fugitive and living in secret in fear of the opposition. The banned leftist politics had made him fight for his life in every moment, and there was no place for a feeling like love there.

Jennifer had shown him that there was another life, another philosophy outside all these. This world was not only for the animals living in the Jungle, but it was also meant for the humans, where there was the existence of virtues like forgiveness, humility, selflessness and friendship. David respected Jennifer, and this respect had created a love for her inside him. Jennifer had a huge contribution to David's rise and power. Whenever he looked at her, he felt better. It seemed to him that Jennifer was a poet herself. She knew that in David's life, poetry must be an unknown term. So one day she asked him in a joking way, "Tell me, David. Do you read poetry?"

"What do you mean?"

Jennifer laughed and said, "I should've asked if you have ever read rhymes?"

David understood her fun this time and smiled. "My favourite poet is Jibananda Das."

His answer made her eyes round with surprise. David said, "I read Marx-Engel, Lenin, Hegel, Feuerbach, Ricardo, the French Revolution because of my political background, and outside of it, I had Jibananda's poems only. After I liked him, no other poet could satisfy me. His poetry collection is my friend since my college life." Jenny listened to his life story with fascination. The more she knew David, the more it seemed to her that a marvellous leader had fallen in the wrong side of politics. Although David had done bad things, he had an honest ideology. The Divisive Leftist politics and the leader's stubbornness had affected many promising young people like David. There was no way for him to return. He would not be returning to a healthy life anytime; someone else would kill him and sit in his place. This was the rule of the circle. Death accompanied every change here. It was only David who had broken the rule and forgave Jahangir because Jenny's words touched David's heart. His sensitivity moved Jennifer too, which she did not understand then. It took a long time. When she looked at him, she found herself thinking of a clear river, lost in a thirsty desert suddenly. The river could never return to its source. Jenny thought that the only way to get David out of all these was to flee from the country. But she could never tell that to David. David was the river that built its own way. Jenny could do nothing but flow with him in her little boat. At this moment, in the beautiful Ashulia Resort, she wanted to tell him something. David, do you know that you are a poem yourself? The poem that my favourite poet has written? But she could not say. After a while, David took out a packet from his pocket and placed it on the table in front of Jenny. She asked, "What's there in it?"

David replied, "Time."

"Do you mean that time is sold in boxes these days?"

"Just see it for yourself."

"It won't fly away, will it?"

"Maybe not, but it'll disappear in eternity."

"You speak very beautifully."

"I hardly like to speak."

"That's precisely the reason."

David laughed out aloud. "I also order murders. Those words aren't beautiful certainly."

Jenny could not find what to say in reply.

She opened the packet. Inside, there was a watch.

"Oh, God! It must have cost you a lot."

"Of course. Nothing is valuable like time."

His sense of humour charmed her even more.

"I am now tying this valuable time in your hand."

Jenny excitedly gave her hand to David and said, "Go on. Put the watch in my hand yourself."

David looked at her hand for several moments, then stared deeply into her eyes and said, "It's a sin to touch a woman's body without touching her heart first."

Jenny was really surprised.

What did David just say? Where did it learn something like that? Jenny understood that David was the man for whom she was waiting her whole life. She blushed, and David looked at her face without saying anything.

Aslam came to stand near them at this moment. If it were not something really important, then he would not have come, especially when Jenny is with David. These days, David discussed many things about the circle in front of her. At first, he used to move aside when these talks arose. One day Jenny told him that she wanted to know about these things, so if David did not mind, he could talk about the circle in front of her. David used to feel awkward at first. The circle had a dialect of its own, which was not easy to speak when in front of an educated and learned girl like Jenny. David gestured for Aslam to come nearer.

Aslam obeyed and greeted Jenny.

"Sit down," David said.

Aslam took a chair and said, "Kana Faruk has taken control of Arambag Pacific Club. He's expelled our Ratan and Munna."

As soon as David heard this, his expression changed, and his jawline hardened. The biggest gambles in Dhaka city took place in Arambag Pacific Club, where every night a huge amount of money was handled. Ratan and Munna from the old Dhaka ran the place on behalf of David. It was clear that Dastagir wanted to bring David to open conflict. David picked up the phone angrily, intending to call Dastagir. But Aslam stopped him, saying, "No, boss. Don't call him now."

David's hand stopped in the middle of pressing the buttons. His face was reddened in anger, which Jenny did not see before. She felt afraid because it seemed that David could do anything right now. He looked at Aslam and said, "Listen, Aslam. There's something that I haven't told you before. Dastagir had used Kana Faruk to murder comrade Bimal Das. You know who Bimal das was. He was my teacher. I'll take revenge now; I'll bring Dastagir to justice…"

At the same moment, poet Anindya Akash was listening to David's angry words while lying on the bed on the second floor of the building, a pair of earphones popped in his ears. The parker pen that he gave Jenny as a gift was now lying inside her handbag, beside the watch that came from David. The pen's powerful sound transferring capability made everything loud and clear. A robin was whistling someplace near, and the poet could hear even that. Jenny loved green. David must have taken to someplace natural.

# Chapter 19

After some time the poet was seen to be descending downstairs, shouting excitedly. He knocked on Jahangir's door, which opened almost at the same moment. The poet said in a happy voice, "Our job is done, Jahangir Bhai! Just listen to what I've found."

He took out his phone and played the voice clip that was recorded in the voice-spying app. It was the conversation between David and Aslam. As Jahangir listened to the clip, his face started to brighten. He said, "You did a great job, poet."

Anindya Akash's expression suddenly turned grave. "It's nothing, Jahangir Bhai. It's only the starting. I'll get the key to the castle; you make preparations for the attack."

Jahangir could not do anything against David inside Dhaka. His popularity had made him a legend, and no one wanted to stand against him. His network had spread throughout the country. The international drugs cartels were keeping contact with him because he had his men in Chittagong and Mongla seaports. Especially the Thai and Vietnamese cartels were sending invitations to him continuously. However, David did not attend these meetings himself, Kibria was sent in his place.

As a result of David's rise, any criminal in Dhaka felt proud and strong to call himself his man. Jahangir could not avail any advantage in Dhaka, so he had planned to bring men from outside. Choto Jakir was pouring money with both hands to re-establish Jahangir. He knew about what Jahangir could do. He was dreaming that he would be the Ward Commissioner of Mohammadpur if Jahangir returned to power. For the benefit of Jahangir, he spread his area of work from Basilia to Washpur to Panchdola. People coming from the outside could live very easily in these areas in the disguise of garment workers. Jakir's men started a boarding house business in these areas with ten houses. Every day, two or three people coming from outside of Dhaka were arriving in these places as ordinary garment workers. Jahangir needed men who were brave and cruel. Gani of Sherpur, the leader of inter-district highway robbers was an old friend of Jahangir. He sent his five able robbers. These people rode the buses in the inter-district route as passengers and then compelled the driver to stop the bus in a convenient place and robbed the passengers of their money or valuables. They were so ruthless that if any passenger delayed in obeying their commands, they would stab him in the chest. Each one of them could be Satan himself.

Jahangir also had a long-standing friendship with Kalyan, the head of Yaba trade-in Maheshkhali. He had sent three men whose occupation was to rob the trawlers in the sea and kill the fishermen. The coastguards were active in the sea at this time, so they came to Dhaka instead of sitting idle. The dreaded robber of Sundarbans region, Shiru had come himself with his people to Dhaka. Many robbers of the Madhupur, Gafargaon, and Haluaghat region were now living in these houses. Jahangir sometimes met with them, told them about their purposes. In the underworld, relations were evaluated by the work. Through work, power and fidelity are proved. Job repayments are also paid by works. These people from out of Dhaka were basically in need of shelters. Now if they worked in Jahangir's service, they would have many advantages in the future when Jahangir would become circle boss. Sometimes they might have to come to Dhaka to hide, and no other place could be safer than Jahangir's shelter in Dhaka. They all roam around Dhaka city all day and return one by one in the evening. They gathered around Janata tower in small groups, ate peanuts and surveyed the surroundings with keen eyes. Jakir had given some new responsibilities to the most reckless ones from his hijacking team, but he did not disclose anything about it to the others. In different points of Dhaka, many beggars with different types of disabilities earned their livelihood through begging. They convinced the mass people by showing their problems and disabilities, and some of them earned more than five thousand takas per day. There were some men to monitor these professional beggars. They were also instructed by Jakir to remain alert. Ratna from Agargao slums was in control of the biggest group of hermaphrodites. Although she was a blind supporter of David, her opposition leader Soheli was with Jakir. Most of the hermaphrodites were actually men in disguise, covering themselves in women's cloth to harass the general people and extort money from them. No one messed with them, so it was easier to deliver weapons and drugs using them.

Jakir met with Jahangir every night when he smoked marijuana with the poet on the second floor of his building. Jahangir found out everything about what was going on in the city from him. The poet had forbidden him to use mobile phones because location tracking and eavesdropping through the mobile phone network were really easy these days. He urged Jahangir to sleep early tonight. They had an important meeting tomorrow.

# Chapter 20

Comrade Dastagir was sweating since he heard the audio clip. He was sitting in a room engulfed in darkness, and trying to make a list of things that David might do now. Dastagir's name was nowhere in the murder case of Bimal Das, and the case itself has pushed away behind other unsolved cases. David might inform the media, in which case his only witness would be Kana Faruk. This problem might be solved by removing Faruk from the story. But if David took the matter personally, then it would be a problem. He considered Bimal Das as his teacher and guru. Bimal was also affectionate towards him like a father.

David might do many things out of that anger, so he should not be poked for now. Dastagir had to keep his head cool and use the characters in the story against each other. Jahangir was alive, and that was his biggest relief now. It was indeed a truth that nothing could be termed as a definite ending to something in politics. Dastagir was benefitted from the death of Jahangir, now Jahangir's survival will also favour him. Jahangir wanted to return to power. Dastagir wanted to remove David, and he knew that Jahangir would do the job for him. He just had to keep calm and watch everything coolly. The Arambagh Pacific Club had to be released for now, until the completion of Jahangir's work. This was the first time that someone raised a finger towards him for the murder of comrade Bimal Das. If someone put this issue on the hand of the opposition, then there would be even bigger problems. He was already in trouble because of his mediocre performance. These days everyone including the capitalists wanted to blame the leftists, using them as the scapegoat. It had to be ensured that David never got near to the opposition.

Dastagir felt a little relief now. He took a little break before pouring the sixth peg of vodka because six was his limit. Vodka needed to be enjoyed in limitation. Otherwise, it could make you an animal. Dastagir had let go of many things from Russia, except his favourite brand Russian Standard Gold. His favourite vodka was made according to an ancient Siberian recipe, from the winter wheat. The first sip of his last peg suddenly made him nostalgic, taking him back to those lively days of Moscow State University. He never touched alcohol back then. But one day put a wager of finishing a bottle half full of vodka without lowering it from his mouth. The second chapter was opened in the hospital. He vomited the last drop of water from his stomach and still wanted to vomit more—a terrible experience. After seven days, when he returned from the hospital, he felt a determination. Vodka wanted to eat him alive; now, he was going to teach it a lesson. Dastagir almost smiled, thinking about those youthful days.

After finishing the last peg, he decided that he would call David now. It was his creative thinking switched on by the sixth peg and was much needed. At some other moment, he would think twice before calling him. But the sixth peg made him skip over those thoughts. David received the call after five rings.

"My son, my comrade. I know that you're angry, and that's quite natural. I never thought that Kana would create such a nuisance! I've warned him after I heard and ordered him to let the club go within twenty-four hours. This is the problem with these illiterate people, you know. Once they taste power, they just go blind. Cannot think about what to do and what not. Fucking assholes don't understand that everything has a chain of command. Send your men to the club, David. And bury the past. Okay, my son?"

David remained silent for a couple of moments before answering, "Okay, boss."

Being addressed as 'Boss' by David was enough to lighten Dastagir's mood. Everything was okay until now, no problem anywhere. Now he had to finish the remaining business quickly.

The place was named Ikuria, beside Dhaka-Mawa Highway. Business tycoon Asad Sadeq had a bungalow here. But no one from around knew who was the owner of the vast property, only that someone really powerful lived here. Once a thief was caught inside. He did not know that the inside of this property was guarded by ten German Shepherds. The dogs had torn the poor thief apart. No one dared to come near to the place since then. There was a big pond inside, in which no one threw a net for over ten years. The fishes became monstrous in size as a result.

The owner had the hobby of angling. He came here once or twice in a month, caught fish, and then enjoyed the barbecue.

Comrade Dastagir sometimes became a guest in this house in total secrecy. 'Bourgeois' businessman Asad Sadeq was his friend from student life. Their friendship had become stronger through some business deals. They did not have any plans for fishing today, however. Dastagir was here to finalise his main plan with Jahangir.

"Who's the girl with David?" Dastagir asked.

Poet Anindya Akash answered quickly, "My girlfriend."

"Really? I thought David had kept her as…" Dastagir grinned without finishing the sentence. The poet became enraged. He said, "Your plan doesn't have any chance of being successful without Jenny's help."

He said it to establish Jenny as an important character, but Dastagir put it in a wholly different way.

"Of course, no trap can be prepared without a woman. Can it, Jahangir?"

Jahangir, being ashamed, lowered his head. Dastagir roared with laughter. "So you can get shy too?" It was Subrata Kundu's wife, Sharmimala who told Jahangir's David's whereabouts. Jahangir took Subrata's wife as his woman after killing off Subrata.

Sharmimala earned Jahangir's faith by acting of being in love with him. Then as the perfect time arrived, she got him to drink a drugged coke, and inform about David. For this reason, Jahangir did not have anything to say in answer to

Dastagir. The poet knew this story, because one day, after being drunk, Jahangir told him about the incident. Dastagir thought that the poet also used his girlfriend as a bait for his own sake. It was worthless to describe Jenny's innocence to them. How could they understand how far he would go to get Jenny, how much crueller he could become? Jahangir had not found that out yet. Jahangir thought the poet to be the Maznu who went mad in love with Laili.

"We'll not take too much time. The first thing to do is to finish the job. And it has to be done with the highest power. Faruk will be there with his full backup. The sooner Faruk knows about when, where and how to work, the stronger his backup will be."

Looking at Jahangir, Dastagir said, "Now your job is to decide how and where to finish the job. Take Faruk's number."

One of Faruk's eyes was completely white, where he once was hurt by a shotgun pellet. Since then the term 'Kana' or 'blind' had been attached with his name. He forwarded his phone to the poet. The poet saved his own number there, then called his number from Faruk's phone. He could not look for long at Kana Faruk's face. There was something in him that made one cringe. He was known as the Hangman for the atrocities he committed in the southern part of the country. Dastagir had gone towards the pond with his hand on Jahangir's shoulders. The darkness was not too thick outside, because the dying moon in the sky was trying hard to spread some light. Kana Faruk and the poet were sitting face to face.

They were not talking. The poet could not find any words. Dastagir and Jahangir could be seen as shadows in the half-light, half-darkness. Surely some secret plot was being discussed, which Jahangir would never share with the poet. There was no problem with that because the poet also had something secret that he would not share with Jahangir. In this dark farmhouse, four men with murderous intent were planning such horrific plans that could terrorise even the devil himself.

# Chapter 21

"Your life story's more exciting than cinema. The more I know about you, the more I feel that you're playing with death and life at every moment, don't you ever feel tired?"

"Nope. I love this game."

David laughed.

"I'm a student of literature, and now I'm teaching language and literature. One reason I came to Bangladesh was to learn more about Bengali language and its literature. But now I think my first literary work will be writing your biography."

David said, "You'll have to wait some more days to write a tragedy."

"Why? Can't I write a biography without tragedy?"

"Yes, you can. But your readers won't eat that."

Both of them started to laugh.

This corner of the Sky home restaurant was very much favourite to Jenny. From here, the green horizon of Dhaka could be seen. Aeroplanes taking off from the airports, the sun setting in the evening, and the night of Dhaka could be enjoyed very much from here. As long as David stayed in this restaurant, it remained closed for general people. The owner of the restaurant got a lot of benefits in his business deals from David, so he was always happy to welcome David in his restaurant.

David wanted Jenny's company. Jenny created unrest inside him. He never felt this attraction towards any other woman. David lost his mother at an early age. His mother's face was a hazy memory to him now. But the intense love that he felt for his mother made him respectful to other women. This characteristic of David was known to everyone. Where the underworld deals were involved greatly with sex and drugs, David kept himself carefully separated from these two. Inside, David was still idealistic. A great comrade like Bimal Das was David's guru. David learned from him the basics of communism. Political power, position, money, strength and could not touch him at all. He lived a poor life, but he was respected by the mass people like a King. It was really easy for him to become MP or minister if he changed his ideals just a little bit. He would have been in the position where Dastagir was now. Whenever David remembered Dastagir, his face became hard. He understood that Dastagir was making some kind of plan now. David's popularity was a legend now, and it made Dastagir angry. By forgiving Jahangir, David had taken himself to a different height, where no other boss of the circle had reached till now. And the reason behind this rise was the woman who was sitting in front of him. Whenever he looked at Jenny, he remembered his mother for some unknown reason. There was no logic behind this feeling. Still, it was the reality. He had tried a lot of times to tell Jenny about it but failed. It was not something that could be told to others. His thoughts were interrupted by Jenny's voice. "David, don't you ever feel like getting out from all this?"

David became absent-minded for some moments. Stirring the soup with the spoon, he said, "The road to crime is a long corridor with a lot of doors. The criminal has to open those doors with his own hand, and once he enters a door, it closes automatically behind him. He's to move forward by opening the doors one by one, and he can never go back. Some try to break those doors in an effort to go back, and maybe break one or two of them. But it's never enough for him. The only way that remains for him is to move forward until he meets with death. It's true that I can break a number of doors if I tried. But my men are like my family, my companions since a long time ago. They all will die if I flee from this. So it's impossible for me to get out from here."

Jenny was waiting to hear this answer. She was a British citizen, she could help him to leave the country if he wanted.

But David did not have any plan like that. It was his inherent leadership that prevented him from doing any such thing.

She asked in an effort to change the topic, "Who gave you this name, David?"

David smiled and said, "My grandfather used to call me Daud. But my father changed it to David. My full name is Iftekhar Hasan David. My father used to call me King David. He used to tell me stories about the king who was victorious against the oppressive ruler Jalut."

"You're a real king now, aren't you?"

"Maybe. But my father didn't want to see me as the king of the underworld, that's for sure."

"You may have become that, but aside of you is getting enlightened slowly."

"That's because of you. You've taught me to forgive."

"Yes, and I was supposed to love you in return."

"Did you keep that promise?"

"What do you think?"

"I don't know. I can only tell you how I feel."

"How do you feel?"

"When I look deeply at you, I remember my mother."

# Chapter 22

"It's dead."

"What do you mean?"

"It doesn't have any charge left."

"Shit! What'll happen now?"

"We've nothing to do."

"Don't talk nonsense. What do you mean by we've nothing to do? Do something for god's sake."

"Well, I can do one thing."

"What's that?"

"I can call jenny and say, "Jenny, my darling, did you know that the parker pen that I gave you, it transfers all the conversation between you and David to me? I listen to them very carefully and become emotional. But the problem is, it's out of power, so I cannot hear anything anymore. And Jahangir Bhai is also in trouble now, because his plan to murder David is being interrupted. "Will you please recharge the pen? Please? Shall I tell her?"

Jahangir looked at the poet with angry eyes. He could not take these funny remarks from the poet right now. He said hotly, "How dare you to make fun of me!"

Though Jahangir's angry expression made the poet afraid at first, a few moments later, he managed to take control of himself. The poet knew how much important he was to Jahangir.

"Cool down, Jahangir Bhai, cool down. Don't you have any sense of humour? I was just joking, nothing else. Don't try to show your temper with me, and don't forget that without me, you're nothing but a big zero in this fight to take the city back. David is much stronger, more powerful now, and do you know the reason? It's because of Jenny's with him. And my poems are with Jenny. They are so powerful that even Jahangir was saved from death by my poems. Do you understand now why I'm so daring?"

The words of the poet Anindya Akash were cold like ice. Jahangir gradually took hold of himself. He knew that he did not have a word to say against what the poet said. Jahangir knew that to get David within his reach, he would need Jenny, and to get Jenny, he would need the poet. On the other hand, the poet did not want to enrage Jahangir, too. This mutual interest brought both of them together to 'compromise' and calmed them. To ease the situation, the poet said, "Have patience, Jahangir Bhai. Why are you so worried when I'm with you? I'll find a way quickly. You want the control of the city, and I want the control of Jenny, and we both want them as soon as possible. I'm getting ill day by day now, you know? See, my forehead is burning."

He took Jahangir's hand and put it to his own forehead.

"See? Can you feel the fever? But this is no ordinary fever, and I think you're burning from this fever too. Yours is a fever for power, and mine is a fever for love. We both are ill now. Do me a favour and make two Shaltus quickly. Meanwhile, I'll write a poem."

Jahangir started to do as he was asked like an obedient student. The marijuana was kept in a packet under the mattress of the bed. Jakir brought this variety of marijuana from Assam, especially for Jahangir – green in colour, and intoxicating in scent. Sitting at one end of the bed, he cut the marijuana into pieces with a scissor while looking sideways at the poet. Anindya Akash looked somewhat abnormal at this moment, like a man burning from fever. He was writing something on the paper attentively. What did he gain by writing all these? But it could not be said that his poems were worthless, because only because of some words David had let Jahangir go, and the girl supposedly learnt those words from those poems. So these poems could not be thrown away; they had many advantages. Jahangir thought that he would not be angry with the poet any more. When he completed making a stick, Anindya Akash said, "Light that, Jahangir Bhai. I want to recite the poem to you while smoking that."

Jahangir took a match and lit the cigarette filled with cannabis. Inhaling a long stretch of smoke, he handed it over to the poet. The poet kept the smoke in his lungs for a long time, then let it go slowly. Emptying his entire lungs, he said, "My writing is finished. Do you want to listen or not?"

Jahangir said enthusiastically, "Yes, I'll listen."

"This is a poem written from my illness. Listen then."

*My fever is gone this time*
*Without your kisses.*
*A new history is written*
*After all illnesses.*
*With green eyes and blue blood*
*You think yourself an Aryan*
*But you are not exempt*
*From the limits of my poem.*

"Tell me, Jahangir Bhai, how did you like it?" the poet was now asking an ex-circle boss, the notorious Jahangir to critique his poem. The thought made him want to laugh out loud, but he suppressed that and stared at him.

Jahangir could understand only the first two lines of the poem. My fever had gone away without your kisses. It seemed marvellous to him. He said, "Do kisses work as paracetamol?"

It took a while for the poet to understand what Jahangir meant, then he started to laugh. He laughed like a madman, and he's laughing turned into coughing after some time, then he laughed again. Jahangir looked surprised.

One or two puffs of the cannabis were enough to intoxicate the poet. He was laughing like this because he was already high. After some time, he stopped. The cannabis-filled cigarette kept being handed over until it was finished after a few minutes. Many people lovingly called marijuana by the name Shaltu. The poet said sadly, "Love, love's everything. Understand that, Jahangir Bhai. Love's behind every creation. You love power, so you want to kill David, and I love Jenny, so I want to kill David. We both are lovers, although we are united in the question of hating David. What a surprise, isn't it. Jahangir Bhai? How do love and hatred reside in the same heart?"

# Chapter 23

Jennifer could no longer pay attention to her classes. Her mind flew away in the middle of lectures, and she could not remember the most trivial things, fumbling for the necessary words. This had never happened before. If this situation continued, her students would surely guess that something was wrong with their teacher. She had to be more alert. Already she had gained a reputation as a teacher, and she was also popular among the students. An attractive figure, British nobility, Cambridge University's degree – she had captured all elements of worldly charm, but still, she held no pride. She was a person who liked to stay as an equal to everyone. And her biggest beauty was her simplicity. Whoever came closer to her was influenced by her personality. The things that were happening these days were affecting her personality. Today, she was teaching Othello, a tragedy by William Shakespeare, Othello, the Moor of Venice. Black, Muslim moor Othello fell in love with the white beauty Desdemona, and Shakespeare had used this relationship to portray the jealousy and racism that engulfed that age. The whole class was listening to her lecture as if enchanted, but Jennifer did not miss the sound of a message alert that came from her phone inside the bag. She looked at her wristwatch. The class would be finished after five more minutes, but she wanted to check the message right now. To spend the time, she wanted to know the student's opinion about this tragedy. One of them started to speak, but she could not pay attention to. She stared at the student blankly, her mind elsewhere. As soon as the class was finished, she opened her bag and checked the message, only to be a little disappointed. It was the poet, Anindya Akash. He was waiting for her in the cafeteria.

"Hey, what happened to you? Are you sick? You've become so thin! What happened? Please tell me. Are you okay, poet?"

Ah! Life seemed so beautiful to Anindya Akash when he saw Jenny's anxiety about him. He gazed at Jennifer without blinking, at the woman for whom he could burn this city to the ground.

"God knows, you're starving for how many days!"

Jennifer hurried to the cafeteria counter, as usual, to bring food for the poet. Akash looked at her from the behind. She was beautiful from behind, from the front, from left, from right, from the sky and from the ground. Did he miss any angles? Suddenly a poem came to his mind. He took out a pen and paper from his bag and wrote it down. As Jenny returned with a tray full of food, she saw him sitting with his writing materials. She almost jumped in excitement to see that, and said, "Oh my God! Did you just write something?"

The poet handed the paper to her, and Jenny started to read aloud:

*"When I look right,*
*I cannot see my left*
*When I look forward*
*Everything behind me remains hidden.*
*But, when I close my eyes,*
*I can see you in every direction."*

The simplicity and depth of the poem touched Jenny. The lines shook her from inside, and she looked at the poet with unwavering eyes. The hungry poet was eating Tehari, with so much satisfaction as if it was a long time since he ate something. He could feel that Jenny was looking at him, but he could not raise his eyes to look at that innocent stare. The poet hid his eyes using the food as an excuse. At the end of the meal, Jenny said, "Take care of yourself, poet. You've to live a long time in sound health. You have a lot to give to this world. If you are not well, then who's going to make us listen to the songs of morning birds? Who's going to make us hear the sound of leaves falling and waves of water! Tell me, poet!"

This time the poet raised his eyes, and said, "I'm in so much pain, Jenny."

Jenny felt a pang of sadness for the man sitting in front of him. She leaned forward and said, "I understand your suffering, poet. But remember that distance can be beautiful, too. Distance is cosmic. Distance keeps away destruction. Look at the universe, and you'll see that each planet is situated in an immense distance with a strong attraction for each other so that the solar system can survive forever. Enjoy the distance without suffering, poet. Without the distance, would it be possible to write all the poems in the world? Tell me, poet. Would it be possible?"

The poet looked away.

Jenny pleaded, "Won't you look for once into my eyes?"

But the poet knew about the danger of looking into her eyes. Eyes were like a mirror, where the secrets of the heart are hidden. He could not show those secrets to Jenny, because he knew that she had that power. So, to distract her, he turned and asked, "So what shall I do now?"

"You'll create, poet. The creation will be your medicine. Don't you understand that my mind grew up reading your poems? I live in them, and they have created the love for David inside my heart. It was you who brought David to me. Your poems are in my whole existence, and I live inside your poems. I am nothing without them. If your poems live, then I'll live, too. And the death of them is also the same for me."

This time the poet looked straight at her eyes and said, "And you are the inspiration of my poems. I hold you inside them."

Jenny replied, "And I hold them inside me." The poet understood what she meant to say. She did not hold him inside her, only his writings. He has come face to face with the truth. And the more he stood in front of it, the stronger his passion became stronger. The passion for getting her.

# Chapter 24

Several notorious gang leaders and terrorists of Dhaka had suddenly started to come out of jail. Among the 23 terrorists who were at the top of the police list, some died in the crossfire, some left the country and entered other countries of the world including India. And the others were still in jail. Generally, the political governments tried to bring them out before the national election. But it was unusual for them to come out at this time. None were to be found after their release, they all had gone into hiding. David felt worried because it seemed that something was going to happen. He met with everyone in the circle personally and alerted them. The main reason behind his worry was, those who got released never wanted to come out of jail because of fear of the crossfire. Those who helped them were all on Dastagir's side.

There was a time when Dhaka city was ruled by the Seven Stars and Five Stars group. They divided the city between them. After one of them looted a supply of smuggled gold and conflict between the two groups ensued. They broke down ultimately, and new groups emerged – among which Python group, Tiger group, Panther group, Cobra group were most active. They made Dhaka into a city of terror through continuous murders, extortions and kidnappings between themselves. When the media started to become loud, the government had to invent the 'crossfire' theory. After that, the circle came under a central command. At every age, the men in power needed some kind of circle to keep themselves more powerful. In capitalist politics, the main source of money was the circle. Vote manipulation, the siege in the polling booths, and keeping the areas under control was carried out by the underworld. Almost all the MPs – be that from government or the opposition – had some connection with the underworld. Haidar Muntasir was a leader of the same party, but he was active against Dastagir. Once upon a time, his son used to rule Dhaka's underworld. When Dastagir's pet media started to highlight the fact everywhere, Muntasir was replaced by Dastagir with his clean image.

Haidar Muntasir had found out that David was fighting a cold war against Dastagir, and he recognised his chance at once.

If he could put Dastagir out of the picture somehow, then he was the second choice for that post of minister to his party. And David also realised that if he wanted to fight against Dastagir, he had to find someone equal beside him. Haidar was in a tight position in the city because of David. If he found out that David wanted his help, then he could revive his dream for being the home minister again. He had some old deals with Tunda Mirza of Savar, too. Mirza got the job of supplying construction goods to a megaproject because of Haidar. Getting the job without paying any commission, Mirza had a weak spot for Haidar. Haidar believed in favour in return for a favour because it improved relationships, and increased dependency and faith. Haidar knew about the connection between David and Mirza, so he asked him to arrange a meeting with David. Mirza had a 'fun house' beside Dhaleshwari River in Savar and a huge pond beside it. He had a special attraction to hermaphrodites. He used to bring them into his funhouse and watch them dance and sing. But that day he got them away from the house in order to keep the meeting secret. Muntasir arrived in a truck owned by Mirza, and David arrived with his people in two trawlers, through Dhaleshwari via Buriganga. None of them wanted the news of their meeting to reach Dastagir. He could not be given a chance to be alert.

Haidar had not met David before, but he hugged him like an intimate friend as soon as they saw each other. David did not like this extra intimacy from politicians. However, Haidar seemed like a man who did not go around with dirty intentions. This person would respect the business dealings. David liked to talk without any diplomacy, and as he knew that politicians could be really tiresome before they reached the point, he started talking straight. "Tell me, Haidar Bhai. What's in it if I do something for you?"

"The biggest reward would be my friend, dear David."

Like an expert chess player, Haidar got the air of David's intention from the first move. David replied immediately, "I'd appreciate that, Haidar Bhai. At this moment I need intelligent friends rather than powerful friends. It seems that you'll fit my criteria."

"Then let's begin without any further delay. Kana Faruk is the main criminal in comrade Bimal Das murder case. There was no witness, so the case got drowned. However, the biggest beneficiary from this murder is Dastagir, who was once the complainant and is now the godfather sheltering the main culprit, Kana Faruk. Newsworthy of a million, and it can stir the high command very easily. But the news alone wouldn't work, we'll have to get Kana Faruk and make him talk. You must know how to do that. I'm giving this responsibility to you. My job is to finish off Dastagir. I believe in doing a favour in return for a favour. I have no past with you, so there is a question of a traitor ship. Our deal is new, just as our friendship. But whatever's new today becomes old tomorrow. If I become minister tomorrow, then I'll need my old friend, Accountant David. Stop Dastagir before he stops you. He knows your pattern of gameplay. If he's clever, then he'll vanish Kana Faruk right now. And if he's a fool, then he'll try to use him against you. Ultimately, he'll take the path that his fate has selected for him."

David said, "It will be hard to make Kana Faruk talk, but not impossible. I'll have to do it myself. And after Dastagir has lost his power, you'll have to give him to me."

Haidar nodded and said while polishing his glasses, "Dastagir might be comrade to you, but he's nothing to me. You'll decide what to do with him; I won't stay between you. I don't want to murder him, just kill him politically. And if I become the Home Minister, then you can't kill him."

As soon as he heard, David raised his head to look at Haidar, his eyes burning.

"Don't you think that if an ex-minister is murdered when I'm the Home Minister, it'll ruin my image? But there's no need to be tensed. You cannot murder him, but there's always some kind of accident."

Placing the glasses in front of his eyes, Haidar looked at David intently. David felt that this man was surely intelligent, and his intelligence would take him very far. He liked this man.

Mirza was barbecuing an Aieer fish caught from Dhaleshwari River, which was almost seventeen kilograms in weight. David and Haidar – both were very dear to him, so he did not want to miss the chance of being a host to them. Mirza's funhouse was built on the banks of the river. Due to the tight concrete that was used to keep the bank steady, there was no scope for it to break and fall into the river. The two-story Duplex house was situated in a plot of almost five bighas. There was a huge balcony on the first floor, facing the river. Standing there, the horizon could be seen across the other side of the Dhaleshwari River. The food table was arranged in this balcony. Besides the fish, Mirza had organised for more than fifty items. Haidar joked with him playfully about not arranging any hermaphrodite or Hijra dance. Mirza knew that David did not have any interest in these things. Basically, Mirza had kept an eye on David's likes and dislikes. This man seemed really curious about him. He was a circle boss, but there was no affinity for wine, woman or partying in him. A natural solemnity surrounded David always, and he initiated a mixed feeling of fear and respect inside others. His personality was unusual and incompatible with the other circle bosses before him. After the dinner was finished, Haidar and Mirza indulged in idle conversations about the hermaphrodites' sexuality. On the excuse of making a phone call, David stood up and stood near the balcony. The sun was setting fast on the horizon. The birds had started to return home. A flock of teals could be seen flying in the distant sky. He could smell the scent of autumn in the gentle breeze. He had not seen such beautiful scenes for a long time. He felt very lonely, and just then he remembered Jenny. A sigh of relief came out from his inside. How did she get involved in his dangerous life? The girl did not think of consequences; neither did she ever contemplate that she loved a man for whom it was unbelievable to be alive at every coming moment. Those who would come to kill him, they would kill her too if she was with him at that moment. But she never seemed to take it seriously. At this moment, standing in front of the setting sun, David felt that he would have to watch such a sunset with Jenny beside him.

# Chapter 25

David did not have thought about whether a girl could be called without any reason at three o'clock in the morning. He thought that Jenny was asleep, and the phone would be ringing beside her head. For security, he called her through Viber. But he was surprised when Jenny received the call on the first ring. She said in a sleepy voice, "Hello?"

David was at a loss at what to say. Jenny said again, "Hello."

"Sorry to wake you up."

"I'm still sleeping, and I'm talking to you in a dream."

What was the answer to this, David did not know. He remained silent. In that silence, they could hear the sound of their breathing.

"If you remain silent this way, it'll break my dream. And if the dream breaks, my sleep will break too, and for the rest of the night, I'll not sleep. And if I don't sleep, then I wouldn't be able to take classes in the morning, and if I cannot take the class…" Now David understood that she was joking with him, and he laughed, stopping her in the middle of her speech. Fascinated, Jenny thought she could see him smiling with her eyes closed.

"Why aren't you asleep?"

"Two types of people who remain awake in the night. Can you say what kind of people they are?"

"I can say, the devil and the devotees to Allah. One's thoughts are to hurt people, and the other's thoughts are for people's welfare. Both of them don't allow themselves to sleep. So they remain awake, and we ordinary people sleep in the night. And when we wake up in the morning, we start walking on the path shown by any one of them."

"Then it must be the devil who woke you up this late night."

"No! You're not that person anymore. From the day you learned to forgive, no matter who you are, you're not the devil. Forgiveness is the quality of Allah."

"Perhaps I won't be able to do it, Jenny."

Jenny noticed that this was the first time David called her name.

"Why?" She asked.

"I've to be unforgiving once more. I've got a confrontation coming with the killer of my teacher. I cannot forgive him."

"Will, your teacher, gain anything if you are unforgiving?"

"Yes he will, my teacher's soul will have peace."

"How will you give his soul peace by giving up your soul to Satan, David?"

"I'm not giving up my soul to the devil's hand."

"Surely you are doing it, David. You're surrendering yourself to the devil to kill one of the evil persons. That's the devil telling you to be unforgiving. The revenge moves in a circular way, and one falls prey to it after another. Revenge stops only at the door of forgiveness. It is not possible for ordinary people to stop it. And those who can stop it must not be someone normal. He must be someone wonderful, like David."

"How do you have such a high opinion of me?"

"Because I saw you. I've seen how a firefly sitting in the dark is yearning for the light. I am that proof of that yearning in you. Otherwise, the events in the National Park jungle that day couldn't be overturned only by my words. You must understand that the forgiveness you showed that day had taken you to a new height."

"I understand."

"What do you understand?"

"I understand that two types of people wake up and talk on the phone night. One of them is devout; another is the devil."

Jenny laughed out aloud. The strange sound of her smile spread through David's senses. They spent the rest of the night talking. The sound of dawn's prayer call came from a mosque far away. Jenny had created a conflict inside David. He did not know how to forgive the killer of his beloved Bimal Das. He did not even know whether he could forgive him at all. He also thought about how Jenny will think of him if he could not. Reckless David now cared for a person. He was surprised in this change inside himself. Sometimes, Jenny seemed to be much more human; otherwise, why would her words create such a commotion inside David, why would they touch his faith in this way? They not only touched him but also built trust, a kind of aloofness that was being created inside him day by day.

The 18th-floor office of Janata Tower, lucrative lifestyle, dark empire, arms, money, political power, fear, respect – it all seemed valueless to him sometimes. David once dreamt of an ideal world, but he reached the wrong destination while running behind a mirage. So, like Dastagir, he could not change himself completely. The absence of Bimal Das still made him sad. Jenny had found that most delicate and secretive spot inside him, and touched it with a magic wand. David was not able to deflect that touch. He had learnt about the power of forgiveness. Nobody thought his forgiving nature as a weakness. His 'forgiveness' had become popularised in the underworld like the power of an emperor. His enemies disliked him, but even they could not hate him. They avoided him but did not ignore him. Those who did not pay respect did not disrespect him either. David said to his men, "Forgiveness is power," they did not realise it but were surprised to see it be true in reality. They called David a boss, but their respect was like towards a guru, a leader, a commander. So when Jenny talked to her father about David, she said, "Listen, Dad. The man I love is a gangster. He rules the city."

"What're you saying? There are gangsters in Dhaka? Does he look like Al Capone, the Mob Boss from Chicago?"

"No, Dad. He's more than that. I think if he were born in 356 BC, then his name would be Alexander the Great. And if he were born in 1769, his name would've been Napoleon Bonaparte." The father and daughter had a world of fantasy and legends, and while discussing anything, they could easily enter into that world. Jenny believed in playful conversations with her father. Her father also responded similarly.

"Napoleon and Alexander, who looted other countries, were also a type of gangster. There's no reason to glorify them. The Italian mafia boss Al Capone had come to America and followed the footsteps of his ancestors by being a mob boss. And listen, since you've finally liked a gangster, this means he will have all the ingredients to be loved by you. I have faith in you. So, congratulations, my princess."

"I love you so much, Dad, because you believe in me blindly."

"I love you so much, too, my daughter, for your strong morals. My blessings are with you so that no impurities of this world touch you." So far, David did not try to touch Jenny's hand, not even with his eyes. Women learn to read men's eyes like a book. When David looked at her eyes, he looked deeply. His dark, hazel eyes perhaps looked for something, which was not the Jenny of flesh and blood, but something else. That day he said that he found his mother inside Jenny. This confession made Jenny even more vulnerable to David. From then on, fear came to reside inside her. She was afraid of losing David because his life was a terrible battlefield. He had to step cautiously at every moment. Though he was the king of this city, his opponents were active in every direction. It could happen at any time. This fear had eaten up Jenny from inside for many days. She would never be able to ask David about leaving everything only for the sake of a relationship. David was like the torrential river that would surely reach its destination.

# Chapter 26

According to Jahangir's instructions, Jakir had brought two Chakma girls from a beauty salon to give a massage to Anindya Akash. The poet first confirmed that the girl was not Garo, but Chakma from Bandarban. Then he tested their palms to see if they were soft. Then he laid down in the bed and asked one of them to pull his toes, and another to massage his head. The girls were trained, massage therapists. But they have not accustomed to these weird head and toes massage techniques. Winking at each other, they started to work. After all, they had to spend time working on their payments. The head massage girl suddenly pulled his hair a bit stronger. The poet got angry and said, "I'm demoting you. Go to that side and pull my toes. He pointed to the other girl. 'I give you a promotion. Come and message my head." The change worked this time, the girl was massaging with her hands, and the poet had a comfortable look on his face. Occasionally, he recited new poems. The girls listened and tried to hide their smiles. The poet asked with his eyes closed, the poet asked, "Do you know me?"

When they did not say anything, he said, "How'd you know? I'm what you call history. Contemporary doesn't know what history is for tomorrow. The people after a hundred years will know me, not you. You should consider yourself fortunate that you are massaging history. This way, you have become history, too. Massaging history is also a part of history. After a hundred years, there'll be a discussion on the poetry of Bengali literature. There'll be a discussion on me. When they talk about me, they'll discuss about both of you because you have massaged me today. Do you know what they'll say?"

The girls started to laugh again, this time openly. The poet said, "The discussion will be that poet Anindya Akash was so non-communal that he preferred Chakma girls instead of the plain Bengali women to repair the pain in his body. This non-communal spirit of the poet had enriched his time."

The poet opened his eyes and sat up on the couch. With a sweet smile on his face, he asked them, "Don't you feel pride hearing this?"

The girls nodded and smiled. The poet said happily, "I like your silence and smile."

Suddenly the door was opened roughly, and Jakir entered the room like a storm. He said, "You need to come to the boss' room, it's urgent." Winking once at the girls, he turned to leave. But the poet's voice stopped him. "Stop! Remember not to enter my room without knocking in future, okay?"

Jakir looked at the poet as if he saw a ghost. He could not believe that someone could live at his house, enjoy all the facilities starting from money and raise his finger at the owner. Two boys stayed 24 hours on bikes, ready to run errands and everything else for the poet and Jahangir. Jakir himself once hijacked, led the gang fights, and now he was the boss of the biggest hijacking syndicate in Dhaka. One could talk to him in such a way while living in his shelter, was still beyond his comprehension. He was enraged, opening the door and leaving like a storm just as he entered. The faces of the two girls had become ashen. They knew Jakir very well. They knew how cruel this Choto Jakir was. However, Jakir became calm with a few words from Jahangir. When the poet entered Jahangir's room, buttoning his shirt, he saw that Jakir was grinning. Seeing the poet, Jahangir said, "Are you feeling better now, poet?"

The poet said, "Don't teach them only to misbehave. They'd do well to learn some respect."

Both Jahangir and Jakir laughed. Poet Anindya Akash felt a rage inside him, but he did not let it express in his face. The poet knew that they were tolerating him only for their benefit, and at the end of the job, it won't take a moment for them to turn their eyes. The poet fully understood the game of this line now, and he really enjoyed playing it. Jahangir assured the poet in a calm and friendly voice, "Jakir will never make such a mistake again."

"Everything's almost done. Those brought from outside of Dhaka have been deployed to different points. Gupibag Ward Commissioner Nata Babu is with me. Thirty people from Babur will be ready and fully loaded. Janata Tower's not far from Gupibag. Some equipment is still missing. Blackie Naresh is waiting on the other side of the Border with two ready deliveries. The border is hot now, because of the killing of a Bangladeshi farmer by BSF."

"How many weapons are in those two deliveries and what types?" the poet asked.

Jahangir said, "Fifty local made 9mm in each."

Jakir added, "We had plenty of 9mm bullets, but there was a shortage of guns."

The poet asked, "Anything heavy?"

Jakir said, "Bringing heavy weapons from the other side of the border is troublesome. We'll have to make do with whatever's in our hand. Twenty-five to thirty shotguns, ten Mark 4 and six Abul Kalam." The poet looked a little surprised. 'Abul Kalam?' Jakir and Jahangir both laughed at his expression.

Jahangir said, "It's the name we use to call AK47s."

The poet said, "The arms shouldn't be in one place."

Jahangir said, "That won't be a problem, Michaels won't disturb us. Dastagir will handle that."

The poet said, "No, we cannot take any risk. Even if the police or RAB didn't take any action, David's circle wouldn't be sitting idle, and they could snatch away everything, too." Jahangir looked at Jakir, as if to say, see how much intelligent the poet is? With Michaels on their side, they did not think about the other party. The poet could not explain without paper and pen. So there were some A4 papers and a few pens always on the table. The poet rapidly drew the map of Central Dhaka with five points drawn around the Janata Tower. Then, like an experienced general, he said, "We've to divide all our weapons and people into two parts. One of those parts should

114

be kept in these five points. They would be the reserve force. And the other will work as the striking force, moving from the action point. We'll take the original striking force. The most experienced men would be with us, and the rest would be the men of Jakir and Nata Babu, who'd be ready at their respective points. As soon as they have the signal from us, everyone will move towards the Janata Tower."

Jahangir and Jakir were fascinated to watch the poet's planning. They saw it as a blessing to have him at their side. "There is still a big thing left to do," the poet said.

Jahangir asked, "What's that?"

"Dastagir's own faithful people shouldn't be able to stay around us during the work hours. After work, they'll come. It has to be settled in advance with Dastagir otherwise; if Dastagir has a bad intention, he might do it from the beginning. That means we'll play, but Dastagir will take the medal. These games are very common in the history of politics. Pakistanis had lost to the freedom fighters, but it was the Indian army who was declared victorious. So be very careful about Dastagir."

Jahangir said, "I'll manage Dastagir, it won't be difficult."

"That's the real work."

"What is the name of the queen of your hermaphrodite army?"

Jakir answered, "Soheli."

"Make this Soheli Madam of yours meet with me. On the day before the action, our weapons will be delivered by them everywhere."

Jakir was impressed, and said, "Wow! Great plan."

The poet smirked and asked, "What's the nature of your relationship with her? Physical or non-sexual?"

"What are you saying, brother poet? Soheli is actually a man."

"Yes, I know that too. Jahangir Bhai also knows, but we must know how deep the relationship is."

Jahangir laughed, and Jakir, being ashamed, lowered his head.

"It's a matter of faith. How much can we believe her?"

Jakir said with a serious look, "Hundred per cent."

"That means the relationship is both physical and mental."

Jakir quickly said, "No, no. I have a wife, you know."

The poet was trying to hide his smile very hard, but Jahangir started to roar with laughter.

"Well, okay, I think Soheli can be trusted. But before that, I'll have to interview her."

Jakir said, "She'll come tomorrow to meet you."

"But understand this, I'll find out how deep the relationship is between you and Soheli after the interview. If you're lying now, then I'll tell this news to your wife as a punishment."

Jakir said in a desperate voice to Jahangir, "Please, Bhai, make him understand."

"The poet is right," said Jahangir. "Such an important work cannot be trusted to Soheli without interviewing her first."

"Okay, I have no problem if you want to verify her."

Jahangir became serious now and asked, "But where will we get David?"

The poet quickly answered, "That's the next question, but there's more work left to do before. Finding David is my job. First, ensure that my plan is implemented completely. Then bring weapons from India as soon as possible. My work will start after that. What would I do with David if you're not ready?"

The message alert suddenly rang in Jakir's phone. The poet became silent. Jakir read the massage and with a bright face, said, "Jinjira's Liton's been caught."

Jahangir excitedly said, "Where is he now?"

"In Mijamizi of Siddhirganj," replied Jakir.

"Tell them to be careful. We're going tonight."

The poet asked, "Wasn't Liton, your guy?"

"Oh, yes. One of my old companions, and was my near too. But David had put something in his ears that turned him against me."

"He can't be blamed. No one wants to stay in the sinking ship."

116

"He entered this business through my hand. I did everything for me. There's something called gratefulness."

"Is there anything like that in this business?"

Jahangir realised the hidden meaning. Changing the topic, he said, "Your plan includes a big part of the city. How will you tie it together?"

The poet felt great because Jahangir was in his control. It was good to know that he could fight with David directly. It felt better to go to war in this city, very secretly; and there was a poet at the root of this huge incident. Sadly, no one will ever know about his great power. Only one woman came to know that. That woman, who just loved his poetry, surrendered to his poetry. Got fascinated by the power of his poetry, but she could not see the power within the poet himself. The poet felt even better because he was just as powerful as his opponent. After all, David relied on the power of poetry, too. David was following what Jenny said, and Jenny was following the poet blindly. Bravo, Mr Poet! Anindya Akash felt a deep satisfaction, and a smile spread through his face. Jahangir and Jakir were looking at him.

The poet came back to the subject and said, "The thread that I will use is a message, and in that message, there'd be a secret code. Which will be informed 48 hours in advance. Every team leader will come out as soon as they get the message and start to move towards the Janata Tower. They'll fight their way forward if necessary The Tower must be reached at any price. Then we'll take you to the 18th floor. I'll inform Dastagir, who'll introduce everyone with our new Accountant, Jahangir. It'll be history because you'll be the first to take that position for the second time."

It was not a dream anymore to Jahangir, because as the poet spoke, Jahangir saw everything happen before him. Now he could understand that this poet had tremendous power indeed. He knew how to make imagination real. Now it was clear that Jennifer also used this power on David, and he let him live. The poet seemed really dangerous and shrewd. His enemies would suffer, that can be said for sure. Jahangir was thinking of all this, when Jakir asked, "What code will be written in the message?"

The poet said with a smile to them, "The message will be – Jenny Darling, Love You."

# Chapter 27

The local government leader Ishtiaq Munshi could not save Liton. Jinjira's Tokai group had caught him from his in-law's house. Liton had been caught almost fighting. His pistol went empty. Otherwise, it would have been more troublesome. Quiet, calm Mizmiji was shaken by the sound of bullets and handmade bombs. For the past few months, Liton was living in Mizmiji instead of Jinjira. Because, after starting work for David, he started to get threatened continuously. So he stayed during the day in the Jinjira area but went to Mizmiji at night.

There is a group of young boys in Jinjira, most of whom were born in slums and were addicted to drugs. They would do anything for some money. Jakir had given money to these boys, five 9mm pistols and some promises. It was enough to turn them into cruel monsters. They started a competition of showing cruelty in order to be a hero in front of their Jakir Bhai. Liton shot three of them wounded, but could not stop them.

Liton was now hanging from the ceiling in a small room. The room was situated in the roof of an abandoned house in Muktajhil. When Jahangir reached there, it was 2 am.

"Your luck has turned against you, Liton," Jahangir said. You left me to join David's team when he beat you. Now if I beat you, you'll leave him and return to my team again. And if you do that, David will beat you again, and he'll kill you this time. The problem is, David's stupid, so he likes to forgive."

Liton, from his hanging position, said in a very clear voice, "No, Bhai. David is not stupid. He didn't make any mistake by forgiving me. He bought me with his forgiveness. It's not possible for me to go against him. I know that you'll kill me with your own hands because of leaving your team. I'm ready for that."

Surprised, Jahangir said, "If I forgive you now, will you work for me?"

"No, Bhai. I promised David that I'd not go against him in my life."

"I'll kill you if you're not in my team."

"I know that. I'm ready."

Jahangir's anger and surprise were increasing continuously.

"If you kill me, I'll die with my loyalty."

"Still, you'll not join my team?"

"No. I cannot do that. And one more thing, Bhai. David has forgiven you, so you shouldn't have plotted against him. An ungrateful person can never win."

After hearing this, Jahangir turned around to look at the poet Anindya Akash. The poet smiled a little and looked away.

Jahangir's head was on fire after seeing his smile. His insult had now turned into anger. He slapped Liton with all his power and said, "You've betrayed me, too. Haven't you?"

Liton's nose was bloody, but he did not look shaken by that, as if he did not feel any pain. He said in that indifferent voice again, "No, brother. I haven't betrayed you, and it's impossible to survive in this line without being under some supreme power. You didn't have the power so that you couldn't give me shelter. And without a shelter, how the business of drugs is possible?

"I have got the power now."

"But I'm under David's pardon now, Bhai. Your power cannot buy me anymore."

Jahangir had reached the end of his patience. There was already a hammer in the room. Folding his sleeves, Jahangir took the hammer in his hands. Liton started to read Kalima. Jahangir wanted to shake off the humiliation that he found in being forgiven by David. Jahangir started hammering from the feet. Liton was reciting continuously, "La Ilaha Illallahu Muhammadur Rasulullah," and the gross sound of breaking one bone after another resounded with his recitations. Jakir had also put a hand with Jahangir. He was using the broken leg of a chair to beat Liton's legs from the other side. No one was attacking his head yet. Jahangir wanted to give Liton the severest punishment before he died. The hammer was now breaking his rib. The poet did not like these scenes at all, so he went to the other side of the rooftop and lit a Shaltu. He had learnt that cannabis was becoming legal in different states of America, which increased his love for the drug even more. Liton's voice could not be heard anymore, only the muffled sounds of the hammer hitting hard on flesh. The poet craned his neck a little and saw that Jahangir was fixing his hammer on top of Liton's head, ready to strike. The poet looked away. Liton's head burst open with the sound of a coconut being cracked. Jahangir's shirt and face got covered by the splash of blood. He came out a few moments later, unfolding his sleeves and trying to rub away the blood. Coming to stand beside the poet, he took the Shaltu from him and finished it.

A huge moon in the corner of the sky had emerged today. The Poet and Jahangir were looking at the moon, their hands on the railing. After a while, Jakir came out and stood beside Jahangir. They stood bathed under the magnificent charm of the moon.

# Chapter 28

Whenever Aslam walked into David's office on the 18th floor of Janata Tower, he saw him standing in front of the glass window, looking forlorn. He looked like he was in deep meditation. Aslam did not want to give him the bad news in this way, but there was no way to avoid it. So he called.

"Boss."

David replied without looking back, "Tell me."

"We've found Liton's body."

David turned around slowly.

"Where?"

"Siddharganj."

David sat down and waved at Aslam to sit on the chair next to him.

"Now it's evident that forgiving Jahangir was a mistake, boss."

"Your problem is you see only what's in front of you. Try to see who's behind this front. The person who's getting the job done with Jahangir could use anyone for his work. Since using Jahangir has the advantage, he is using it. Do you think that Dastagir would've been sitting around if Jahangir wasn't here?"

"Now I can see that, boss. I made a mistake."

"Jahangir had died on that day. Now he's a puppet on someone else's hand. His days are numbered."

"Understood, boss."

"All the responsibility of maintaining Liton's wife is ours. How old is his child?"

"Ten years."

"Deposit enough money in their bank for the next fifteen years of each month's expenses."

122

"Okay, boss."

"Without Dastagir's favours, Jahangir could not do this. Now, Dastagir's to be stopped as soon as possible. To do that, first, we've to get Kana Faruk."

"Our men are working. It's as if Kana Faruk has disappeared suddenly, but that's highly improbable. Someone must've informed Dastagir that we want to catch him."

"That's not the case. Dastagir knows where his weakness is. And he also understands that I know about it. A clever enemy knows where his opponent could hit him."

"Dastagir can also murder himself. There wouldn't be any problem then."

"If he thought so simple as you, he wouldn't be Dastagir today."

Aslam understood why his boss said this. He lowered his eyes guiltily.

"But your point is half right, Dastagir could do this. But if we only work on it, the other half will become dangerous. We want Kana at any price. Don't just cover the whole country's network. Alert all our people who work at the airport. Keep your friends informed in places easily reachable from Dhaka, like Kolkata, Dubai, Bangkok, Singapore and Nepal. Remember that this is a question of our existence, Aslam. Don't make any mistake."

"Don't worry, boss."

"As long as Dastagir's brain is thinking, we'll have to be worried."

They looked at each other's eyes. Aslam understands the meaning of his boss's last words. Aslam nodded and stood up determinedly.

"Okay, boss."

When Aslam left his room, David slowly got up and stood in front of the glass. The midday sun was shining golden in Dhaka's sky. David realised the fact when talking to Aslam. If Dastagir's weakness was Kana Faruk, then who was David's weakness?

David's enemies would surely want to use his weaknesses to hurt his weaknesses. Suddenly David felt an unknown pain inside him for Jenny. David himself was the reason for her danger, why didn't he think of this before? He read somewhere that love brought foolishness out of people. He laughed at his thoughts. His thoughts and world were divided into two parts now. Jenny covered one of them. No, maybe more than that. Because Jenny's ideas were now useful for him to run his dark empire, Jenny said, "One day you'll see your positive thoughts illuminate your world. Then no one will think of the underworld as full of darkness. You, Will, Be the Sun of the underworld."

Jenny laughed. It took David a while to understand the meaning, but then he also smiled. "The world of criminals will be called the illuminated world. Where did you learn to conjure up these weird thoughts?"

"It's because I live in a weird world. Lots of books have taught me to think quickly and deeply. I can turn a sliver of thinking into the Amazon jungle within a moment. We are fascinated by this genius of writers. We lose ourselves in the world of their thoughts. A talented writer is a player who plays mind games. Literature is nothing more than the trick they use to create their worlds. I want to be a player like them."

"You are already that."

"No, it'll take some time. I've to understand you more deeply."

"What is the relation between understanding me and becoming a writer?"

"There's a relationship because I'll start writing with your biography, but not a biography in the true sense. It'll be a fiction based on fact. I'll write this book in English so that people from all over the world will know about the story of a firefly called David who yearned for light. Just a few moments ago, I got the name for my book."

David said in a surprised voice, "Really?"

With a sweet smile, Jenny said, "Yes."

David excitedly asked, "Can I know the name now?"

"Well, I think if I should tell you the name now or keep it as a future surprise."

"I have no confidence in the future. I live for the present."

Jenny pointed her finger towards David and said, "I have a little difference with you. I live in the present for the future."

"I can never argue with you."

"Why do you even try?"

David laughed aloud.

Jenny was impressed to see that smile. After a long time, David laughed from his inside. This smile, in some way, turned him into another man. A dark cloud of anxiety left him. He said with a sigh. "I feel a lot lighter now. What happened to me, Jenny?"

"Perhaps you are smiling many years later."

"How do you understand all this? I really don't remember the last time I laughed."

"After a long drought, the first rain creates a scent on the ground. And whoever smells that can understand that it's been long since it rained."

"You can express your feelings in Bengali very well, which is surprising. You're really beautiful."

His eyes looked at her with deep love. Jenny could not look for long at those eyes; she dropped her gaze down. A water coaster went through the Hatirjhil, leaving a long wave behind. The waves spread and started to break down on the side.

After being alerted about the safety of Jenny, they did not meet twice in one place and did not use the same cars twice. David did not keep too many people with him to be noticed. Aslam, Kibria, Johnny and a trusted driver followed him like shadows. Today they were sitting in a deserted place in Hatirjhil. They were immersed in each other's feelings. There was no need for words anymore. They fumbled for words that could be said out loud, but could not find any. After a long time, David broke the silence, saying, "What did you decide?"

"About what?"

"Whether you want to let me know the book's name?"

"Maybe so. I think a person who lives in the present should know the name now. Life is fragile, we never know what'll happen to us tomorrow. At least the person about whom I'm writing a book should know the name before. I'll name it – 'The Son of Underworld'."

David believed that for everyone, there was a chance to change their life. He became the circle boss and met Jenny at the same time, on the same day. It was as if fate had sent the empress and empire to him at the same moment. He did not understand it so far, but gradually, he perceived that his and Jenny's destiny had been tied together. He started to want Jenny but did not know how this could happen. He was accustomed to getting everything he wanted. Any beautiful girl in this city could be his if he just wished for it – be that with money or with power. David's reputation was like the celebrities, even the country's top heroines wanted his company. The relationship between the underworld and the film industry was nothing new. Any heroine's career would get a huge boost if she had a connection with David. But he was never attracted to anything like that. His respect for his mother created a respectable position for every girl inside his mind, and he had either respected them or stayed away from them. Besides, there was no time to worry about these issues in his already risky and troubled life. But Jenny had come and opened up a strong river of emotions. David had started to think that Jenny was a part of his destiny. But he did not understand how to get her, and what would he do if he got Jenny. Maybe they would stand in front of the large open glass window of the 18<sup>th</sup>-floor office of the Janata Tower, and watch the sky. He would show Jenny how the ugliness of life got blurry from this height. This was the convenience of looking from above. As human beings made their home, as women cooked, would Jenny also do something like that? But she does not have to cook, because everyday meals would come for David from the renowned restaurants in Dhaka. He would arrange it for Jenny, too. Would Jenny take part with him in controlling the circle? Would she join in the murders and gang fights? Here David's thoughts came to a stop. David returned to reality and suddenly asked Jenny. "We're actually two persons from two different worlds, isn't it, Jenny?"

Jenny quickly responded, "That's why we're attracted to each other, like the two magnetic ends of the earth. But if you're a magnet, then I'd happily become the iron."

"I can say that too."

Jenny joked, "You're David, the Circle Boss, and you can say whatever you want. If you want, you can look at the eyes of the killer, and then you can cry like a baby."

Without being able to understand her joke, David became serious and said, "I didn't understand that part."

Jenny laughed with the sound of glass bangles tinkling and said, "Those words are part of a poem. They suit you very much. It seems you are the person of that poetry. You seem to be saying the words."

Assured, David asked, "Can I hear the poem?"

Looking directly at David's eyes, Jenny recited,

*"I can look at the eyes of the killer if I wish*
*If someone asked me to bow my head*
*Or, at any moment, I can embrace a child*
*And cry like a child if I wanted."*

David said in a surprised voice, "Did you write this?"

Jenny said with enthusiasm, "Oh my God! What're you saying! If I could just write two lines like this, I would've considered myself blessed."

"Then who wrote it?"

Jenny said even more enthusiastically, "His name is poet Anindya Akash."

"Wow! Very beautiful name, Anindya Akash. But it makes me wonder if he is a boy or a girl."

Jenny laughed out loud, and she kept laughing like mad. David looked at her with fascinated eyes. He could not look away from her. Jenny said, "Poet Anindya Akash is a handsome man, not a girl."

"Surely he's a great poet?"

"He must be because he's a great poet in my eyes."

Jenny's face slowly became serious, and she said, "I've become interested in reading Bengali poetry because of his writings. His poetry made me more interested in Bengali literature. He had made me the inspiration for his poetry. I see the ideal world through his poetry." A charm spread over her face, and she said, "The poet loves me."

David joked, "There's no way not to love you!"

Jenny said with a conviction in her voice while looking deeply at his eyes, "I found you in his poetry."

David did not want to miss this opportunity anymore. So he said, "I want to meet this poet."

Jenny was as happy as a baby. She said, "Oh, that'd be really great. I'll see the poet and the poetry together."

"Now I remember, I had to create a birth date for myself when I was filling up the form to attend my matriculation examinations. It could be used as an occasion for my birthday. I don't know when my real birthday is, actually, so there was no question of observing it. There was no such thing in our childhood, and I had a kind of hatred for these things as they belonged to the bourgeoisie or the rich class. Now, do you want to make an occasion using that date? A special person needs to be met with a special day. How's the idea?"

Jenny was excited. "Excellent!" she exclaimed. "It's just perfect."

David could read Jenny very well, and understand that the two of them were thinking in the same plains. So, he created a nice plan inside his mind. He had only one of his mum's memories, a silver ring that his father had put on his mother's finger during their wedding. After her death, this token of their love was kept by David's father. In his childhood, David saw his father many times, crying with his fingers around the ring. After his father died, David always wore that common silver ring in his little finger. That cheap ornament was the most expensive thing in the world to him. Jenny would surely realise its value.

Touching the ring in his finger, David thought, on that special day, in front of her favourite poet, he would give it to her and say, "Jenny, will you marry me?"

# Chapter 29

A thriving prostitution business was run using the hotels, guesthouses, and rented houses in Dhaka. David's did not have any interest in their share of the money, even if it reached the circle regularly. Finally, it had been found out that the last person in this syndicate was Kana Faruk. Gambling, Prostitution and the business of drugs held hands together. Starting from setting up the gambling boards in various clubs, betting in BPL and IPL Cricket T20 – everything was in his control now. As Faruk was in direct control of Dastagir, he used Dastagir's complete power to his advantage. Dastagir thought that David had forgotten about Bimal Das. And even if he didn't, he would in order to become the circle boss and for the sake of working together. But Dastagir could not think that David's response would be totally opposite. He thought he would bring Kana Faruk with David's hand. Instead of that, the matter became complicated. It was also dangerous to talk directly to David about this because Dastagir knew that David would ask such questions about the murder of Bimal Das which he could not answer. Since that day, their distance had increased to such a large proportion that it would never change. Dastagir knew about the condition of David's mind. So he told Kana Faruk to stay undercover for some days. In the meantime, he could manage David. Kana Faruk not only went into hiding, but he also went undercover literally. He went undercover in a burqa. Faruk's relation with the pimp of Tejakuni Para, Mira was not old but already very deep. Due to their relationship, Mira had many advantages in her business. There were no threats from anyone because of Faruk. Mira gave her suggestion to hide in her house for some days. Faruk had a small body, so no one could understand if the person under the burqa was a male or a female. He and Mira roamed around the city of Dhaka undercover in a burqa. Everything was going well this way.

David's men were searching everywhere throughout the city to find Kana, but he continued to do his work wearing the burqa with Mira. Unfortunately, a girl who regularly went to Mira's house caught him first. Mira told her that he was her cousin, coming from the village. But the girl had a relationship with one of the boys from David's Circle. Identifying a person who was blind in one eye was not a difficult task at all. The girl, as expected, described his face to her boyfriend. After that, surveillance was set up in Mira's house for 24 hours. Mira did not smoke, but the price of two or three packets of cigarette was being added daily to her name in the nearby store. David became certain that there was a man inside. After that, the name of Kana's favourite brand of cigarette was found out, and it also matched. Flying a camera drone outside the window of Mira's fifth-floor flat, they saw Kana. He had to be caught as silently as possible because he was so cunning and cruel that he would not hesitate for a moment to shoot if threatened. If they went inside the house to catch him, the risk was bigger. So the plan was to catch him on the street. From the surveillance of several days, it could be established that Kana and Mira generally walked to the street after getting out of the house, then a rickshaw would take them to the main road. From there, by a CNG or taxi, Kana went to Dilshad Hotel in Magbazar. From there he continues his business dealings, though he never came out of the burqa. He made Mira his assistant. When talking to somebody, he whispered at first to her ear, then Mira repeated his words. Kana's preferred weapon was marked three rifles, In the golden days of finishing off the enemy of the people, his trademark outfit was hanging a rifle on one shoulder and the gun belt on the other in a cross shape. But it was not possible in the city. Now he always had a loaded 9mm in his waist, and a spare magazine with it. David cautioned everyone that while catching him, his hand should not reach the pistol in any way because they had no idea about the fierceness and courage that Kana possessed.

The plan was to jump on him from behind. At first, one of them would suddenly fall down and grab his feet hard, and the rest would jump to get him. Finally, the task was completed perfectly. But the problem was, Kana did not utter a word since he was caught.

Everyone was waiting for David in the secret Wire House at Tejgaon Industrial Area. Kana had been kept in complete security and confidentiality. They needed him to talk. There was an earlier order that he should not be harmed in any way. A video message would be made for the media. As soon as Haidar and his lobby's media got it, they would start campaigning strongly against Dastagir. At the same time, a group of barristers were ready to accept the video message as the confessional statement of the main accused in the murder case of Bimal Das and take the old murder case to trial.

Kana was sitting in a chair. His hand were untied so that he looked healthy and normal. His legs were tied with Smith and Wesson leg cuffs, however. David came and sat face to face with him. Kana Faruk looked at him without any expression in his face. David remembered him slashing the throat of one of his enemies. Kana's white, blind eye was staring at him without moving at all, like a serpent's eye. This Kana Faruk killed David's loving comrade Bimal in Paltan. David clenched his jaw and straightly said, "You know who I am. And I also know who you are. I have no disagreement with you, nothing to say at all. All we'll do now is an important job. You've killed Bimal Das according to Dastagir. Why, where and how you did that – tell it in front of the camera."

An iPhone was placed on a stand behind David. He showed it and said, "Look here and start to speak. If you listen to me, I won't kill you. I'll just hand you over to the police. But if you don't, remember that you'll roll on the ground while begging me to kill you. But I won't do that. What do you want?"

Kana Faruk stared at him with his single intense eye, no question or answer in it; only the cold silent gaze of a poisonous snake.

"What do you want, Faruk? I don't have much time."

Kana Faruk spoke for the first time in a hushed, cold voice. "That's true, David. You don't have much time."

Kana Faruk directly threatened him. David knew what he meant, and also knew that it was not only for threatening him. At the same time, he understood what Dastagir wanted. The twenty-armed men standing behind David stiffened as they heard Kana's words.

"I'll give you two minutes to answer, yes or no. You have three ways to go, but two answers."

David took out the Barretta M9 from his hidden shoulder holster inside his blazer, and the silencer from another pocket. He said while putting the silencer on the barrel, "You have another answer, I know that. And that's your silence. Your silence means-no. Of course, you can use your silence, and I'll try to make you talk for as long as it takes. Two minutes is a long time to make a slight decision about saying yes or no. Let's start the game."

At David's gesture, one of the men came forward and put a handcuff on his hands. His pants were folded to the knee. David noticed that Kana was clenching his teeth so hard that his eyes started to become wet. David called loudly, "Aslam."

"Yes, boss."

"Start counting the time."

"Okay boss."

Aslam looked at his phone's watch and said, "Time starts now."

David said in a cold voice, "Faruk, don't be a fool."

The time was passing by the seconds. Everyone's eyes were turned towards the three of them. Faruk's eyelids were shivering. Aslam was looking at the clock uninterruptedly. David tried but could not visualise his beloved comrade Bimal Das' dead face. He could only see the living face, grave and tired of tension. Standing in front of the assassin of a genuine Communist who saw the dream of a fair world, David suddenly thought if the feud between him, Dastagir and Kana Faruk was also a part of their war. Would it cause the evolution of communism? In today's difficult world where 50 per cent of the world's total wealth is in the hands of just one per cent of the world's population, who would build a communist society again? What if all this sacrifice was meaningless and slaving for capitalism was the ultimate destination for all?

"Time's up."

Aslam almost shouted in excitement. But Kana Faruk remained silent and still as a statue. David raised his pistol steadily and placed the barrel fitted with the silencer on his left toes and pulled the trigger. The first bullet pierced the toes with a stifled sound. Kana tried to crane his neck to see the wound, his only good eye bulged in disbelief. Very slowly, David put the pistol a little over the wound and shot again. Kana was trying to withstand the pain by clenching his teeth. The cement floor below his feet was already covered with blood. The third bullet was shot at his shin, the sound made clear that the bone was broken. This time the blood did not gush out of the wound. Kana Faruk's whole body began to shiver, and he bit his teeth, trying to keep silent.

In a very calm voice, David said, "You still don't want to talk, Faruk? No problem, I'll keep knocking at the door of your silence. Let's see how long you can remain silent." The fourth shot hit Kana Faruk's shin just at the middle. Heavy bullets of nine millimetres probably broke his bone into two pieces from the middle. Kana lost his consciousness before giving the last shiver.

"You want to sleep while I'm knocking at your door. But that's not possible, Faruk. Now I'll break your sleep."

David shot the fifth round on Kana's right foot, in the same proportions of his left one. Kana woke up with that bullet, and looked at David with a bewildered stare as if he did not know what was going on. He looked around with the same bewildered look in his eye, looking like a lost person trying to identify the place where he was sleeping. The sixth shot was shot in the left leg, according to the right one. The blood pressure of his body had already decreased, so this time just a white hole appeared on foot. His eyes were full of tears, but the fire was still burning in it. Probably he lost the feeling of pain, and he just looked at David. David shot twice more in his left leg, taking out the bone marrow with the last shot. Eight bullets were emptied on his two legs, but he did not make a sound for once. He had a half-smile in his face, like a madman. With eight bullets in his two legs, he was sitting in front of them, looking around, and sometimes trying to see his legs. David reached for his pocket for a new magazine, but he remembered suddenly what Jenny had said to him to save Jahangir, "If you're forgiving, I'll love you."

Suddenly his hand stopped. How would Jenny react if she saw his cruelty at this moment? This thought made him numb for a few moments. At that moment, Rustam came forward. David had got him out of jail. He said, "Boss, I know how to make people talk. Give me a little chance, boss. You take a little rest."

David wanted something like this. Before getting up, he only said, "Okay, try."

David understood that Kana would not talk. He lost a lot of blood and would become unconscious within a few minutes. He was yearning for some fresh air, so he came out from the closed, damp atmosphere of the warehouse, and stood under a large tree outside. A lot of birds were in the tree, chirping among themselves.

In Rustam's pocket, there was always a slim, long and impossibly sharp steel knife. He kept the knife in a sheath. He didn't like pistols or firearms. He liked to do his job with the knife. Rustam inserted the knife inside the wound in Kana Faruk's shin and wound it like tightening a screw.

David heard a groan from the outside. Rustam seemed to be pretty good in his work. But nothing more could be heard other than that. No further words after that. Aslam came out and stood next to David. He asked, "Any news?"

Aslam replied, "Rustam's trying."

Kibria also came out. David asked him too, "Anything happened?"

Kibria said, "Rustam's trying, boss."

About twenty minutes later, David said, "Let's see what the situation is!"

Three of them entered together inside the warehouse and saw that Kana's one leg was separated from the knee and lying on the ground, and the other was in Rustam's hands. He was trying to open the leg cuff. The head of the piercing ear is tilted on one side. As David stood in front of him, Rustam dropped the leg on the floor and stood up. Kana Faruk looked like an island, surrounded by a sea of blood. Rustam, touching the other side of his hand to Rustam's nose, said to David, "Sorry, boss. He died."

# Chapter 30

The Chakma girls had started to like the poet. They not only heard to him now but talked too. When the poet recited something, they said, "Explain it to us." Then he talked about the poem in really simple language. The girls listened and said, "Its meaning is really so beautiful!" They did not think the poet ordinary now, but a genius, a visionary. They were also surprised because he did not misbehave with them as many other men did. Even when they got nearer to him, he separated himself very carefully. They had found out the poet had a woman. Whatever he wrote – it was for that woman. But one thing remained unclear to them – what was he doing here? He didn't smoke cigarettes but took marijuana, and kept talking hush-hush with these people. They waited for him then. Their payment was on an hourly basis, but the poet gave them more money than that. But they liked the man, so the money was not important anymore. If the poet wanted, they would massage him for free. They thought, how fortunate this woman whom he loved so much was. He was writing sad poems these days. Those poems made Indrapati Chakma and Attadeepa Chakma sad. One of them was massaging his head, and another the toes. And the poet recited in a low voice,

*"For a little love*
*I put myself in danger*
*Who is there like me?*
*Who roams like a pauper?*
*Like me, who else*
*With a fountain of words*
*Looks at your face and*
*Turns into a statue?*

*A thousand people surround me*
*As I hide my sigh*
*I live in silence*
*As time passes by*
*As my heart burns*
*I want to see you smile*
*So I keep smiling*
*In the outside.*
*Who else would love you?*
*As much as I do*
*Who else is there, who…?"*

The poet kept saying the last line over and over. "Who else is there, who? Who else is there, who?" The girls were touched by his gloominess, so they stopped what they were doing and sat silently. He could feel their eyes warm for him. He asked them, "Tell me, girls. Who else is there?" They started massaging again after they heard it because they knew the poet did not expect an answer. With full concentration and affection, they massaged his head, pulled his toes. He started to feel sleepy, but just at that moment, his phone started to vibrate. Opening his eyes irritated, he saw Jenny's name on the screen, and his laziness vanished. He felt an electric feeling running through his nerves.

As soon as he received the call, Jenny asked in an upset voice, "Why did you keep your phone switched off? It's been several days since I heard from you. Are you okay, poet?"

The poet could feel a huge rush of happiness running through him. But he suppressed his feelings and said in a plain voice, "I'm okay, Jenny."

"Don't lie to me, please. I can tell from your voice that you're not okay. Where are you now? What're you doing?"

"Yes. This is called motherly affection."

He looked at Attadeepa Chakma after saying this and saw that her eyes bulged in surprise.

Jenny said, "I have good news to give you, poet."

"What's that, Jenny?"

"I recited one of your poets to David, and he was really impressed. Now he wants to see my favourite poet. His birthday's on 25th December. He has invited you as a special guest."

The poet said carefully, "No, Jenny. You know that I don't like to go to parties."

"It's nothing like you are thinking. You are the only invited guest, and it'll be just the three of us. So relax."

"Then it's okay, I think. But these criminal types scare me, Jenny. Besides, David is the biggest gangster in this city. He has a lot of armed sidekicks. I'll be even more afraid than I am now, and your party will be ruined. Can't you just keep me out of these, please?"

"Okay, I'll tell David not to keep his men around. By the way, you're right. A poet shouldn't be among the armed people. He should have flowers, birds and songs around him all the time. The poet and his poems will remain there."

"If what you're saying is true, then I'll go."

If I tell David, he'll arrange everything according to your taste. He knows very well who you are."

"Who am I?"

"You're that poet, who showed me my David inside his poems."

# Chapter 31

Some monsters were born in this world in human disguise. Kana Faruk was one of them, and Dastagir was the commander of that monster. His mutilated body was found floating in Shitalakhya after three days, both legs gone. Dastagir almost vomited after he saw the condition of the body. The Detective Branch of police sent the pictures of the body to him after they identified it. The corpse had bloated three times its original size by that time, but Dastagir could recognise him easily. He called the operational in charge of DB and said angrily, "You must be joking with me. I don't know whose body it is, but it's not Kana Faruk. Please try to have some sense in your head. If it's him, then where're his legs? Now don't try to convince me that his legs were eaten by the fishes. Listen, Faruk doesn't have any enemies who would kill him. He's an honest and leftist political worker. He's still alive, so find him as soon as you can."

A general diary had been filed in the police station after Faruk vanished, so his political identity now surpassed his connection with the underworld. Whatever happened with him now would be to fulfil a political agenda termed as a plot by the miscreants. Dastagir brought his political identity in order to gain his own ends. If Faruk opened his mouth, then it would be covered as an effort to tarnish Dastagir's political image. But he could not feel at ease until he knew what David did with Kana Faruk for sure.

A monster like Faruk died in the only way he could – because of his terrible obstinacy and pride. A perpetrator to numerous murders, he was supposed to die like this. But he could live a bit longer if he wanted. He didn't believe David and thought that he would kill him after getting his confessions. He could never believe that David could forgive the murderer of his most dear friend and teacher, so he decided to die without coming in any service to him.

Haidar was at first frustrated at Kana Faruk's death, but then he found out the political benefit. He had two ways to move now – one was blackmailing secretly, and the other was using the political benefits openly. It could be said that Faruk had confessed before he died that he killed comrade Bimal Das from Dastagir's command. The evidence would be presented in court when the case moved forward. And the open benefit was a witness was found dead after he confessed about killing Bimal Das and the connection of a minister of the present government in this incident. One side was saying that the body was Kana Faruk's, and the other was saying that it was not him. The media was openly arguing about this. One of the leaders of the government had raised fingers against the Home Minister comrade Dastagir. Faruk was seen with him in his last days in different meetings and public assemblies. And this Kana Faruk was the main culprit of Bimal Das murder case. Haidar was clearly stating in TV Talk Shows that it was Dastagir who benefitted the most after the murder of Bimal Das. David was really surprised at Haidar's cunning. Kana Faruk was dead, but still, he used by Haidar for their benefit. The current gossip in the market was that Kana Faruk testified against Dastagir, so he was silenced.

Dastagir had to fight in both underground and overground now, and the main reason behind it was Kana's confessions. It could not be taken from David if he had it, because Dastagir could not find any reason to ask for it. Kana Faruk had increased the already spreading gap between the two of them. And David knew that nothing was more ferocious than an animal that could not run anymore. Dastagir would try to strike a fatal blow this time. David had to be completely alert because the first blow was really important. One had to make the first strike if he wanted to win.

# Chapter 32

The fog was a lot denser in the river.

A boat was advancing through the river fog and darkness, crossing the Bosila Bridge. The polluted, oily black water of Buriganga slapped the boat's sides and the oars. Jahangir and the poet were sitting on the mat spread over the boat. As they advanced, the lights and sounds of the city started to fade.

"Shall I light a Shaltu?" Jahangir asked.

The poet said, "No. I want to feel like Jibananda in this fog."

"Who was he?"

"You can say that he was someone who craved for feelings. He used to walk the roads of this world for thousands of years."

"Yes, I realise that he was really crazy for feelings. Maybe he smoked Shaltu, too. Shall I light one?"

"Nah, I don't feel like smoking it now."

"Then recite one of your poems."

The poet turned to look at him.

"Wow, Jahangir Bhai! This is the first time you wanted to listen to a poem. You must be in a great mood now."

"Yes, your company has taught me that poems are not actually bad things. Makes my chest feel empty."

After rowing for about an hour, they were already far from the city. The riverbanks were covered by farms, fields and crops now. A sweet, wet flavour could be smelled in the air. The poet inhaled long, and then started to recite:

"*I have a rose in my left pocket*
*And a magnolia in my right*
*So I am not afraid of your*

*Soldiers, tanks and guns anymore*
*Stop this conquering*
*And enslaving*
*This time I will fight you*
*For a pure heart."*
"Bravo."
"Why?"
"I can smell something like power in the poem."
"Bullshit."
"Why?"

"The only thing you can smell is marijuana. Now light it."

Jahangir barked with laughter. These days he sometimes laughed, which the poet had not seen before. He also started to laugh, and seeing them laughing, Jakir beamed too. A marijuana-filled cigarette kept being handed over until it was finished. They had stopped in a sand bed in the middle of the river. The place was very quiet here. The fog enveloped them from every side like clouds, sometimes really dense. The poet remained sitting on the boat, while Jahangir and Jakir stood up and watched their surroundings with watchful eyes. There was no one around. Assured, Jakir took out a small plastic drum from inside the boat. A sack came out of the drum, and several pistols came out of the sack. He arranged them side by side on the mat—five pistols in total, with ten cases of bullets. Keeping the weapons in the middle, they sat down around it. Four of the pistols were nine millimetres, and the other was a small self-loaded semi-automatic colt 32. Jahangir asked, "Tell me, poet, which one do you want?"

The poet replied almost shyly, "You are the expert in these things, Jahangir Bhai. You choose one for me."

Jakir also agreed and said, "Yes, Bhai. You should pick one for the poet."

After thinking for some moments, Jahangir picked up the small colt and said, "Such a sweet thing, isn't it?" He smiled and gave it to the poet.

This was the first time that the poet took a firearm in his hand. The pistol felt really comfortable in his grip, glistening like a bar of chocolate. He handled it with care. Jahangir said, "It's a special one."

The poet added, "To be used for a special job."

Jahangir barked again with laughter and said, "Now it's time to train you." First, he showed the poet how to put the magazine inside the pistol, and how to remove it, and how to ready it for shooting by pulling the slide. The poet learned everything within fifteen minutes. Jakir got down on the ground and fixed a wooden board about twenty yards from them. Jahangir showed the poet how to fix his target before shooting. He was given twenty bullets of 32 calibre. He would use five of them for the practice, and keep the other fifteen for his own safety. After a few moments of preparation, the poet's first bullet reached its target. Jakir and Jahangir appreciated the shot with a few praising words and claps. The poet took some time before shooting again, but when he started, he shot all four bullets within three seconds, and all of them found their target. The sound of gunshots was sucked in by the fog.

Jahangir and Jakir were astonished to see the poet's expert marksmanship on the very first day. Jakir asked in a grave voice, "Have you ever handled a pistol before, poet?"

"Nope."

"Then how could you shoot so expertly?"

The poet started to fill up the magazine with bullets and said, "My pen is more dangerous than this pistol of yours. I deal with canons. This small colt is nothing compared with that."

Jakir had understood by now that the poet never answered anything simply. But he should not be irritated, because he followed his own rules. The war that Jahangir was fighting; this poet was the main commander of that war. The more Jakir saw the poet, the more mysterious he became to him.

On the way back, Jahangir told the poet that everything was ready according to their plans. Their men were divided into two parts and deployed in various points as the poet instructed. Everyone would get their guns and ammunition as soon as the poet signalled. The poet asked after listening to everything, "Do you remember the final message code?" Jakir and Jahangir both nodded.

The poet asked, "Tell me."

They replied together, "Jenny Darling, Love You."

The poet's face brightened.

Something was happening in the city – small robberies and other crimes were almost stopped. The city dwellers might not notice it quickly, but the OC of Sutrapur Police Station thought otherwise. It was unusual, like the silence that dawned before a big storm. Something big was going to happen. He had an old friendship with David, so he decided to call him.

# Chapter 33

Jenny wore that wristwatch that David gave her today, for the first time. She also bought a lovely green Sari for the day. She did not know what David's favourite colour was, but she knew that the poet Anindya Akash liked green the most. She was reciting one of his poems and putting on make-up.

*This evening comes*
*In your green sari and grass*
*Evening star adorns your forehead*
*Gently smiles.*

Jenny's father had taught her to wear a Sari in her childhood. David or the poet – no one had seen her in a Sari before. They must be really surprised. For some reason unknown, it felt like this was going to be the happiest day of her life. She looked really beautiful in the mirror.

Poet Anindya Akash's least favourite dress was Panjabi, but today he had to become a poet and dress like one. So he wore a Khaddar Panjabi and stood in front of the glass. He looked really handsome, and the jute woven bag that he had in his shoulder completed his outfit. No one used these bags nowadays. He used some hair gel to flatten his hair to one side, parting it neatly. He never looked at himself with this fascination. It could be said that he lived in the seventies or eighties when poets dressed like this. He decided that this classical outfit should be retained, so he would wear this dress at least once a month.

The occasion to scrutinise him in the mirror came for the first time today. The mirror was like Jenny's eyes, which was showing him his true nature. David had a lean, muscular body, but he did not know it was enough to win a woman's heart. The beauty that Jenny found inside him and talked about, he could not find that looking at the mirror. Maybe girls had some other way to see that. What else could be the reason for a woman like Jenny to fall in love with David? David was wearing blue jeans and a light cream shirt. His weapon was an inseparable part of his life, and after wearing a shirt, the second thing he did was strapping the shoulder holsters. When he was doing that today, he remembered that Jenny said, the poet was afraid of arms and armed men. He smiled a little inwardly. How someone could write poems if he were afraid of arms!

# Chapter 34

A tumultuous situation had descended upon Dhaka – everyone wanted the murderer of comrade Bimal Das to be punished. Those who believed in communism started marching towards the Shaheed Minar with their red flags. DNA test had proved that the body was indeed Kana Faruk's, which meant that at least half of the accusation was true. Every finger was pointed at Dastagir now. He was caught in a tight situation. However, any meeting with the members of the ministry could not be called without any strong proof, and everything heard so far were speculations. One of the two sides was trying to prove it to be true through their media, and the other was trying to ignore it as the propaganda from the enemies of the country. A lobby inside the government was active to turn Dastagir's reputation as Home Minister, and he kept saying that this was also a plot by them. Within the government, it was an open secret, so they did not do anything themselves but had let the court decide.

This was the good news for Dastagir for now. If time is the best healer, then the court was the best solution. As he sipped the glass full of Russian vodka, it seemed to him that as long as there was Russian vodka, no one could uproot communism from this world. He laughed at his own thoughts because he must have crossed his limit today. He was not called in the meeting with Shaheed Minar today. But even just yesterday he was the sole speaker in any issues related to the murder case of Bimal Das, it was like his own property. That property had gone out his hands today, and even if he was sitting in a powerful position like the Home minister of the country, he did not have anything to do. Haidar grabbed that chance completely. He entered the field with his full power and was trying to convince the high command that they would complete their promise of providing a lawful environment to the people by removing such a person from the position. And the communist leaders took his statements as a green signal from the government. They were also angry at the newly bourgeois Dastagir in the guise of communist, and none of them hid their anger now.

Dastagir looked with surprised eyes at the TV screen. Haidar was giving a speech at the meeting arranged by the communist party, asking for the quick judgment of comrade Bimal Das' murder. The TV camera zoomed out and showed out the meeting premises. Haidar's face could not be seen because of the red flags, but his speech could be heard very well. Dastagir's jawline hardened. He will see Haidar. He knew how to stop a revolution with another revolution, how to bury one issue with another.

# Chapter 35

Due to safety issues, David did not inform them of the name of the restaurant until it was just one hour before the fixed time. The place was in a Golf Club, called Palm Heights. Poet Anindya Akash arrived there at the right time-7 pm. Jenny and David were already there waiting for him. The poet was wearing a Panjabi and a jute bag in his shoulders. He also had some flowers in one hand. He looked completely different today. However, Jenny identified his outfit within a moment – it was the classical outfit of the Bengali poets. He looked really handsome in this dress. Jenny, impressed, went forward to welcome him then took him to their table. The whole restaurant was empty. A grand piano was being played at one side by a pianist, and another person was playing the violin. A renowned wedding planner house had designed this special evening today. The whole restaurant was booked, and the piano and violin were also arranged for this occasion only. David kept the poet's words – he did not keep his bodyguards inside the restaurant; all of them were outside in the parking lot and the nearby areas. He stood up from his chair and shook hands with the poet. Then spreading his blazer in both sides, he said, "You can see that I decided to honour your request, and didn't keep any weapon with me."

All three of them laughed after hearing it, and the environment became friendlier. Sitting down at the chair, the poet said, "Happy birthday, David:

*"All the roses of the world*
*Are for you today*
*I give you the rainbow now*
*And all its colours.*

*I give you a handful of sunshine*
*Even if it's a rainy day*
*The birds are singing for you*
*Because you were born today.*
*Happy birthday."*

The poet put the roses that he brought on David's hands, which he received graciously.

"Thank you so much, poet. I've never felt so special. You brought your poems and red roses for a person like me, which is amazing."

"I actually wanted to bring white roses, but couldn't find it. Witch doctors of the middle age thought that red roses signified grief, and it was for the dead people. It was appropriate only on the coffins. It seems I've made a great mistake because I brought red roses for someone alive. Sorry, David."

David thought that poets probably talked in this way, so he said, "Is this a poem, too?"

Jenny laughed when she heard this. "It's hard to understand which words he says are poems and which are not."

The waiter served fresh apricot smoothie.

David smiled and said, "This is dangerous. A man who couldn't be understood is really dangerous. In my business, we recognise people by their work only. It wouldn't be helpful for us if we tried to measure them from what they said. You must've noticed the politicians; they confuse the people with their elaborate talks."

The poet sipped his drink and asked Jenny, "Don't you understand me, Jenny?"

"I understand your poems perfectly, but not you…"

"Do you understand David?"

"Yes. I can understand him because I understand your poems. If you are the poet, then it's David who is your poetry."

David asked curiously, "May I know what you're talking about?"

Jenny laughed out.

The poet replied, "We're talking about a game, a game of understanding." This time, all three of them started to laugh together.

David gestured for the violinist and said, "I've come to know that Jenny likes the piano, and your favourite is a violin. So I kept only these two instruments with respect to you both. Tell the violinist what you want to hear."

"That's great! You're changing all my ideas about the underworld of Dhaka."

"I can understand what you mean. Those who ruled Dhaka before me, they all arose either from breaking the carrier wagons in Kalampur, from the occupation of snatching in the slums of Mugda, or from the drugs business in Kamrangir Char. This is the first time an ex-communist who has read Marks and Engels is ruling Dhaka, so it's no wonder if you are surprised."

He started to laugh. Jenny could feel a hidden sorrow behind his words, so she asked the poet, "Tell me, poet. What do you want to hear?"

The poet said mischievously, "I don't want to hear just any music. I want to test this musician. Are you ready?"

The violinist was amused at this suggestion and nodded his approval.

The waiters came and served three types of steaks, including beef, chicken and fish.

"Okay. Listen, Mr Violinist, I'll now test your skills. I'll tell you about a scene, and you'll have to enter that scene. You'll take the sorrows of that scene inside yourself, then play it through your violin for me. Can you do that?"

Jenny tried to stop him and said, "Why're you asking him to play something sad in this beautiful evening, poet? Ask him to play something happy."

"No, Jenny. I think it should be as the poet says. It seems really interesting to me. You describe the scene to the violinist, poet."

The poet started to say.

"Listen carefully, Mr Violinist. Think that you are standing in a very old graveyard by the side of a green mountain. In the grave in front of you lies that man who snatched the woman you loved from you. Your heart is pained with both the sadness and anger of losing the loved one. Now your job is to wake up the corpses in that graveyard with the symphony of your violin. Can you do that?"

The violinist sighed and said, "I can try."

He started to play with all his attention and skills, filling up the restaurant with the melancholy sound of a violin. It was connected to the surround system via Bluetooth. The violinist was unbelievably skilled, playing the backup chords perfectly. It was as if the violin was literally crying, and its cry touched Jenny. She could not eat, just kept playing with the food. David thought that the musicians should be given a large tip today. The sad music was making him absent-minded, too. Looking at Anindya Akash, it seemed to Jenny that he was starving for many days. He was eating his beefsteak with relish while rocking his head matching with the music. It could be deduced that the violinist was skilled enough to satisfy him.

When the violinist stopped, the whole restaurant was full of the gloominess that enveloped a lonely mountain valley. The poet clapped and said, "You have passed your test." David also joined him after a moment. Only Jenny, feeling sad, kept herself busy with the food.

Suddenly the restaurant felt too silent after the music stopped. Jenny felt a pang of frustration towards the poet – why did he ask to play such a melancholy tune? Maybe David understood her mental condition because he said, "Now we'll listen to Jenny's piano."

He motioned for the piano player to come forward.

"Tell me, Jenny, what do you want to listen to? But it must be something happy."

This time, Jenny smiled.

She told the piano player, "Now I will test your skills. Imagine that it's a beautiful, sunny day. Suddenly a black cloud appeared in the sky, and it started to rain. There's a big rainbow in the sky, and several butterflies have started to dance to see it. I want to hear that dance of butterflies, rain, and sunshine upon the green grass in your music. Can you do that?"

"I think it'd be easier than the scene you wanted the violinist to play, so I can do it," said the pianist with a smile. Then he returned to his piano and started to play. In the background, the violinist brought sunshine in his music. The butterflies descended on the green bed of grass, filling up the whole world with a strange romanticism. Jenny had an expression of being mesmerised in her face. David looked at her, whose eyes, in turn, were fixed on the poet. The poet was looking at the pianist's fingers. David felt that this was the right moment, but suddenly he was really nervous. This feeling inside himself surprised him, because he had never felt any kind of fear or nervousness in his life, then where did this feeling come from? Suddenly he thought, what if Jenny did not love him but this poet? Would she refuse his proposal then? Jenny loved poetry, so it should be the poet Anindya Akash who deserved her love. What if he made a mistake in recognising her? He felt really nervous, and the poet sitting in front of him seemed to be his opponent at this moment. He didn't know what to do now. The piano was playing Jenny's favourite music right now, and Jenny avidly looked at the poet. Anindya Akash looked at her for a moment and smiled. The sound of a violin that was playing a while ago seemed to have returned. David sighed inwardly and looked at his mother's ring. He touched it. His mother's memory soothed him a little. He came back to reality. He did not care for anyone, and he would never accept defeat. Amidst the piano's music, he said, "I want to tell a story to you now."

The poet asked, "Is it something serious?"

"It's the story of my life, so it must be."

Jenny said with a lot of interest, "I cannot wait to hear it."

David pointed to the ring in his finger and said, "The story is about this ring."

Both of them looked at the silver ring in his finger. David started to say how this ring belonged to his mother and how

153

he came to own it later. Jenny felt an unknown sadness inside herself for David.

David said, "This cheap piece of silver is the most precious thing to me in this world. I want to give this ring one more story." He took it off from his finger and held it in front of the poet and Jenny. Then he looked at Jenny and said, "I want to give this ring to you, Jenny. Will you marry me?"

The poet looked as if he could not believe his eyes. It seemed that the ground below his feet was trembling. What was David going to do?

Jenny's face was bright like a full moon, illuminating the whole restaurant. She was smiling and crying at the same time. David's hand was shaking in nervousness. After several moments, Jenny gave her hand to David and said, "Yes."

Poet Anindya Akash managed to take control of himself very quickly. He gave out a shout and put his fingers in his mouth and whistled excitedly. Then he congratulated Jenny and shook hands with her. He embraced David cordially and held him in his embrace for several moments. The musicians had understood by then what happened in front of them just now. They were also happy to express their excitement in piano and violin. The inside of the restaurant became a full-fledged festival. Jenny did not let go off David's hand since then.

Four Santa Clauses entered with a big cake inside the restaurant. Seeing them, everyone remembered that today was December 25, Christmas. The poet jokingly said, "Wow, today we're celebrating the birthday of two prophets in a single day." David and Jenny did not understand this at first and looked with puzzled eyes.

The poet explained, "Jesus and David."

Jenny and David laughed at this time. There was a birthday cake in one of the Santa Claus' hands, and the musical instruments started to sound the romantic tunes of Happy Birthday. Four Santas, Poet Anindya Akash and Jenny started to sing along with that music.

One of Santa's came forward while dancing and put the cake in front of them on the table. Another of them lit a candle and put it on the cake. The cake had these words written on it – "*Happy Birthday, David*."

David asked Jenny, "This must be your idea, right?"

"What do you mean?"

"I'm talking about the Santas and the cake."

Jenny started to laugh and said, "No, no. I think it was the poet who did it."

The poet blinked and asked, "What're you talking about?'

"Cake, and Santa?" Jenny replied.

"No, it's not my idea either," the poet said.

Suddenly David felt worried. He took out his phone to call someone when one of the Santas came to stand in front of him and said, "It was my idea."

His face was covered with a big white beard, and he had the classic Santa Clause dress on himself, but David could feel that his voice was somehow familiar to him. The man took a pistol from inside of his dress. David could only say in confusion, "Is that you, Jahangir?"

The first bullet hit his chest at the same moment. Jenny screamed. Jahangir pulled the trigger seven more times, emptying the magazine and dashing out of the restaurant. The poet started to scream, "Murder! Murder!" And followed Jahangir at the same time. The stairway was at the end of the passage, and the restaurant was on the fourth floor of the six-story building. The other Santas took the lift to get out of here, but Jahangir and the poet were using the stairs. Jahangir sent a small text message while descending, which said – "*Job done.*"

After reaching the second floor, the poet said, "Send the message code, Jahangir Bhai. Quick."

The message was ready for transmission, Jahangir just pressed the button and sent it to Jakir. As soon as Jakir got the message, he forwarded it to almost a hundred phone numbers at once. The poet asked Jahangir, "Did you sent it?"

"Yes."

"What did the message say?"

"Jenny Darling, love you."

The poet shot him directly at his forehead without giving him any chance to be surprised, bursting his head apart and spraying his brains on the wall behind. Jahangir himself chose this 32-colt pistol for the poet. Wiping the grip with the border of his Panjabi, the poet put the pistol inside Jahangir's Santa Claus dress.

He had to find Jenny and get out of here quickly. The girl must be really afraid. He started to ascend the stairs again, heading for the restaurant while shouting, "Murder! Murder!"

The plainclothes members of the Detective Branch circled the restaurant and waited for the signal from the poet. They started their action now.

A bloody gunfight took place in the parking lot below between the DB police, three of Jahangir's men, and David's assistants – Aslam, Johnny, Kibria and five others. Aslam, Johnny and Kibria were dead, and the others were arrested after being wounded. As soon as the text message started to reach various corners of Dhaka city, fights and chaos started everywhere. The fight was between David's men and Jahangir's gang members who came from outside of Dhaka. Already 130 casualties were confirmed. The news had spread that David was dead too, and it broke his men's wish to fight. Jahangir's men took control of Janata Tower, and Jakir was leading them. At the early hours of dawn, it would be decided who is going to be the next circle boss. Curfew was implemented in the whole city because of this gang war.

# Chapter 36

The next day.

The Home Minister Dastagir was briefing the press about the present situation of Dhaka. He said, it was the most notorious gang fight that ever took place in Bangladesh, which created a war zone out of Dhaka. About 130 known criminals and terrorists died because of this fight between Jahangir and David's gang.

"We are suppressing them ruthlessly in order to provide safety to the common citizens," he said. "Our government has a zero-tolerance policy when the question is about terrorism, and our lawmen are working continuously to withdraw them once and for all. Gang, godfather, and mafia – whatever you call them – they shall never rise again in this city because we have uprooted their main point of power."

One of the journalists asked, "Honorable minister, we know that Jahangir and David – both are dead in the gang fight. We saw Jahangir's dead body, too. However, David is missing. Did he escape by any chance?"

"It is true that we did not find his body. But we are confirmed that he was shot, and his men retreated with him. As one of the witnesses described, David's wound was serious, and he is not supposed to live for long. Our team is working continuously to find him dead or alive."

Another journalist asked, "You are one of the suspects in the murder of Kana Faruk, who killed comrade Bimal Das. Your opponents are also saying that you are responsible for this gang war too because you want to bury the issue of Kana Faruk with this fight. Do you have anything to say?"

"Please don't listen to those who conspire against us. We believe in work, and we are working for the safety of the common people. Let the law do its job. No criminal, no matter how much power he has – shall escape justice. It is true for the common citizens and for the Home Minister alike. Thank you."

Another asked, "Honorable Minister, we have found out that your party is not very happy with you. Is there any chance that you might resign?"

Dastagir said, "My country and my people are much more important than my party. I have never worked to make my party happy. My only motto is to work for my country. So the people of this country will decide whether I will stay as the Home Minister or not. Thank you, all. No more questions please."

David's dead body was removed secretly that night because it had been decided that the circle would not have any new boss right now. A mystery would surround the disappearance of David, and a legend would be made out of his courage, power, compassion, forgiving nature and his larger than life image.

David would be a terror for some. Some would worship him as a hero. He would also become the target for attack for someone. The blame game of politics would blame him for many things. David would run the circle from behind the shadow. And that is precisely what happened. Even after so many years of David's death, some new criminal, calling for a donation from a businessman in the name of David, terrorised the city. So David would live, as a ghost lives. If the fear of the ghost does not reach the people, they would not respect Janata Tower and share their money. If the money did not come, the party would become weak, and unable to run the election cost of the party. If there were no fear, criminals would not be under control. David's fear was indispensable for the capitalist state.

# Chapter 37

Jennifer left Dhaka within fifteen days after David's death. She would never return to this city, where David was no more. Jenny knew that this city had a lot of secrets, and she found them. The ring that he gave her stayed on her finger and probably always remain there. Jenny knew that the love of the poet for her was honest, but his attempt to win her love was not honest. Why did a poet who cannot become poetry himself, write poetry? So before the farewell, she requested the poet not to write poems any more. The poet kept her request and went back to the village, determined that he would never return to this city.

Many years later, a Bangladeshi-British writer's novel had found a place in the New York Times Bestsellers List. The writer was being discussed in the media of Dhaka enthusiastically because the background of her novel was Dhaka. The New York Times wrote in their weekly book review "This is a story where a lovesick poet became a murderer for the love of a woman, and a cruel murderer became forgiving. The name of the novel was *'The Son of Underworld'*."